VIBURNUM GATE

A Nantucket Island Art Mystery Romance

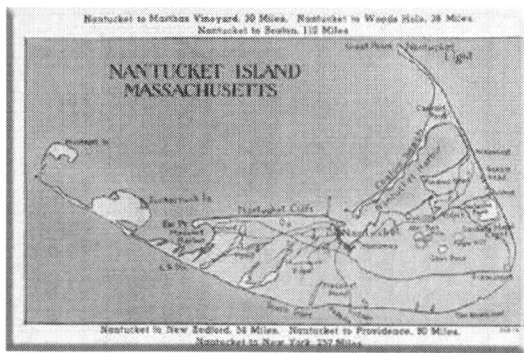

CYNTHIA GALLANT-SIMPSON

Copyright © 2010
Cynthia Gallant-Simpson
Revised February 2012

Cape Cod Cozies & Mysteries, Ink
P.O. Box 1115
South Orleans, MA 02662
Email: hesperus@capecod.net

Printed in the United States

All rights reserved. No copy may be made of this document by any means without the permission of the author.

Cover design by the author

For Ken…as always

ONE

The ferry pulled away from the dock in Hyannis right on schedule, promptly at nine-fifteen. The sea was glassy and although it had snowed the previous night and the wind had gusted up to about thirty-five knots from the northeast, the tempest had left few visible signs of that fast-moving storm. Just a light dusting still snugged up against the foundations of buildings and trunks of trees where it had blown and stuck gave evidence of the winter night just passed.

As usual, except in those rare, aberrant years when Cape winters resembled Vermont, the good old moderating Cape Cod sea air had melted the snow rather quickly. Just enough to add a holiday feeling along with the festive boughs of greens festooned with red velvet bows the volunteers from the Hyannisport Garden Club had hung in the ferry waiting room.

The captain's friendly relaxed voice welcomed everyone over the loudspeaker, insinuating itself into Nora's thoughts of what might await her on Nantucket. Glad of the distraction, Nora switched her daydreams to thoughts of ferry captaining. Not a bad job making the half dozen crossings each day from Cape Cod to the island of Nantucket, Nora mused.

Two hours and fifteen minutes for the regular, slow ferry, the Gray Lady, a brief one hour for the fast ferry, Flying Cloud. Nora chose to take the slower, Gray Lady. Time for thinking; her aunt's attorney would be waiting on steamship wharf and then a trip to his office for her signature, and finally, she'd be free to walk to the cold, closed up house. With only two days until Christmas, the ferry was as crowded as any day in the hectic summer tourist season. Looking around at the high-spirited passengers, she surmised that the majority of these holiday travelers had family on-island and were traveling with laden packs of holiday gifts for those awaiting them at the terminal to drive them to cozy homes decorated in garlands of green with red and gold velvet bows.

Nora felt a pang of envy. This was certainly unlike all of the years she had taken this same ferry to the island to Aunt Bessie's warm and inviting house, to her second home, her island home that had been always there for her to return to whenever she chose. As a child, Nora never gave a moment's thought to the realization that even her beloved aunt was mortal, and that when she went, everything would radically change.

The couple seated next to her, dressed casually but expensively, asked Nora to watch their belongings while they went forward to the snack bar for coffee. Would she like some too? "No, but thanks for asking."

"Well then, how about a bottle of juice, they sell Nantucket Nectars on board and they are *really* tasty?"

"Thanks, yes, sounds good, get me anything that looks appealing."

Leaving her in charge of a laptop, a large shopping bag marked Saks brimming with smartly wrapped gifts done up in bold striped gold and white paper and tied up with wide red velvet ribbon, and two duffel bags she wondered what their Christmas would be like. Gazing around at the passengers' faces, she could not see any expressions of sadness or doubt. Only she had no family members on the island waiting for her or her gifts. She carried only a canvas duffel bag.

Attorney William Macy was a virtual stranger but for their frequent phone conversations following the death of her aunt. He had been kind in his condolences but he was hardly family.

Aunt Bessie had lived on the island for more than sixty years, first as a child summering with her parents and then later, year round after she married an islander. After Nora lost her parents, Aunt Bessie had stepped in regarding Christmas and all other school vacations, including the long, languorous months of summer while her adoptive parents took off gypsying around Europe and the East. They were great people and Nora loved them and was grateful for their sacrifice in taking on a child later in life, a life of freedom, travel and adventure. However, because of Aunt Bessie they were free to pursue their interests in ancient history and obscure artifacts at least when Nora could be sent off to Nantucket. They had often offered to take her along summers, promising an exciting, footloose kind of two months immersed in their interest. Although she found their work fascinating, she preferred those wonderful summer days on the island. Swimming in the clear, cool water just steps from her aunt's little beach shack, sailing her own Opti until she grew too big for it and moved up to a Barnstable Catboat, tennis, hanging out with her friends at Children's Beach; nothing could beat those experiences. The summer she turned fourteen, Aunt Bessie arranged for her to study painting with a renowned island painter, Carrie Mitchell. The class sat at easels at various locations around the island painting *en plein aire*. That was when she decided, definitely, to be an artist, when she grew up.

Her parents' best friends and professional colleagues, the Woodmans, Estelle and Bert, had adopted her, according to an agreement made at the time of her birth in case her parents died while she was a minor. Not morbid, simply pragmatic and caring. No one expected it ever to come to pass and so, it was fun having them as kind of surrogate parents interested in her schooling, taking her to the theatre and opera and teaching her about ancient history and the wonderful finds they brought back from their trips.

If nothing else, her professor parents, Melanie and Aidan Kavanagh, were practical people, to a fault. Bright, efficient, sensible, pragmatic and organized ought to have been both their epitaphs.

They were also affectionate and she had loved them very much. Both of them college professors, a New York Jew and a Boston Irish Catholic who practiced neither religion, both being agnostics with a strong leaning toward atheism, Nora was left to discover her own spiritual persuasion. Not at all shocking them when she, at nine, decided to be a Druid. They bought her books on the subject and took her to meet a friend who studied Celtic history and was an expert on what was known of the Druids of the British Isles. One Christmas they traveled to England so that she could see Stonehenge, Salisbury Cathedral, Oxford and Cambridge (these latter in hopes she might choose to matriculate there in due time) and other important sights as well as the Tate and the British Museum. The trip reinforced her decision to study Druidism and inspired her love of Celtic art.

All four parties signed the agreement that was then placed safely in a bank security box along with Melanie's father's bar mitzvah yarmulke and Aidan's mother's diamond ring; none of the four ever expecting that the agreement would ever see the light of day again. The Woodmans, with no children of their own, although broken-hearted when the Kavanaghs died in a train derailment on their way to a conference in Chicago (both feared flying), delighted in making Nora their child just shortly before her twelfth birthday. They had always been there, like an aunt and uncle but they were busy people, caring and generous caretakers but not family, like Aunt Bessie.

However, now Aunt Bessie was dead and the house would be hers. She had no idea how expensive it was to live on an island where everything has to come across by ferry, no idea of the market value of the house should she decide to sell, and no idea of where her life was headed once she stepped off the ferry. Would the inheritance change things, she wondered? The past few weeks had been a pensive time, full of contradictory, possible scenarios that, to date, had found no satisfactory solutions.

The young couple returned, bringing her a delicious cranberry, raspberry juice drink. "Nice easy trip, have you been on the ferry before? Is it always this calm?" the woman asked. Nora answered that she had, "yes, in all kinds of weather. This is lovely, but I also like the rough sea trips. You get a little of everything on Nantucket Sound."

She remembered making the crossing in winter when the seas were angry, steel gray and battering the lumbering ship. Returning to school just ahead of an October hurricane, following a bout of pneumonia that had kept her on the island under Aunt Bessie's loving care for three weeks, the waves had washed right over the ferry. Based on the dire weather forecast, vacationers headed for the ferry like lemming with suitcases. The packed boat could have been transportation for refugees fleeing some European country during a war. The scared faces and use of barf bags were further indications of the desperate nature of the trip.

Nora did not add these "frills" to her observation. Across the way from where Nora sat, a family was busy spreading out as if they were in their own living room. Although the boat was crowded, there was available a long, low table the family, parents and two young daughters, were able to commandeer upon which they spread out picture puzzles, paper dolls, coloring books, crayons and snacks in a variety of blue plastic containers. These things came, seemingly never-ending, from the capacious satchel sitting on the floor by the mother's legs. A picture perfect family: tall, slim, blonde mother, slightly older father who showed hints of flattering gray in his light brown hair, and two little girls, probably six and eight, blonde like their mother, dressed in colorful leg tights with calico over-dresses. A couple of Pippi Longstockings girls, old-fashioned looking and obviously well behaved.

Nora found it difficult to observe this happy family as she would have liked. Their every movement, every nuance, and every conversational exchange captivated her attention. However, she had to be carefully circumspect so as not to appear to be outright spying on them. However, their close proximity allowed her to eavesdrop on some of their conversations, interrupted only by the general din of the holiday crowd intent on beginning their celebrations early.

Her inclination to watch the dynamics of families often caused her uncomfortable moments. Half a dozen times the mother caught her eye and although she tried to be cool and look away feigning no more interest than a horizon scan, she knew she'd been caught out and marked as a nosey person. She had always dreamed of being part of such a family. The Woodmans had done their duty and there was no doubt that she loved them and they her but they were not really a family, at least in the storybook way that Nora dreamed of being.

The Woodman's home on Joy Street on Beacon Hill was roomy and comfortable and her bedroom had been thoughtfully decorated by Estelle to look just like the one she had grown up in Brookline. Mrs. Maloney, a stout, motherly Irishwoman with a fascinating brogue, newly from Dublin, cleaned, cooked and generally made their lives doable by running their house efficiently. It was she who became more of a mother to Nora than Estelle Woodman. Estelle meant well, but she was not the mother type.

You cannot change a tiger's stripes, make a silk purse from a sow's ear or inject old-fashioned family dynamics into a couple who had always been free to come and go and had purposely not had children so as to insure this freedom. It was Mrs. Maloney who greeted and hugged Nora when she returned from school, baked cookies and Irish bread, and applied Band-aids. It was this surrogate mother figure who reminded Nora to wear two pairs of wool socks under her ice skates as she headed for the Frog Pond in Boston Common. The Woodmans loved her but Mrs. Maloney supplied the things the motherless child needed most, beyond security and physical comfort.

If asked, despite the loss of her dear parents, Nora always replied that her childhood was idyllic. However, it was Aunt Bessie who was the true constant, the center of her Shangri-la, and with her gone, Nora was not sure of much of anything. Being an adult was not all it was cracked up to be if it meant losing loved ones who gave your life a mooring, a safe haven when the storms threatened.

A soft snow began to fall as the ferry swung to face its bow out and begin backing its stern into the landing. Children came running to the windows to exclaim that it would be a white Christmas. Coats were donned, children rounded up, parcels gathered and read newspapers left on seats and tables as was the custom so that returning passengers might avail themselves of the news.

The dock overflowed with smiling and waving, waiting friends and relatives as well as the usual van drivers from the various inns and bed and breakfast establishments, signs in hand, ready to whisk travelers away to their cozy digs. Everywhere, in inns, B&B's there would be fires glowing, bowls of shiny apples by the check-in desk, the resin scent of greens and the joyous sound of taped carols filling the air. Family members jostled one another trying to reach their island relatives; kissing, hugging, exclaiming how the grandchildren have grown and delighting in the loss of front teeth, how little so and so is now walking on his or her own, how healthy everyone looks and how good it is to see them again.

No Aunt Bessie. No battered "Woody" station wagon to drive her around town before heading home so she could to view the holiday decorations along cobblestoned Main Street and the side streets. Houses and businesses so festive that Christmas began in earnest for Nora at that moment. Eventually, they would arrive at the eighteenth century brick house that had been home to Starbuck sea captains for generations. Foursquare and sturdy, standing among equally well-preserved examples of Nantucket's long history as a wealthy whaling town, among other incarnations, the house was home to Nora.

Instead, Nora had made a reservation at the Jared Coffin House at the top of Broad where they have the best, well almost best, breakfasts in town. Arno's holds an equal place for that meal, but they close for the winter. At least at the inn she could just roll downstairs on Christmas morning to join the families who celebrated the holiday there every year. The inn honored its regulars with small, decorated artificial (fire regulations) trees in their suites. The bounteous holiday breakfast was a high point along with Christmas Eve dinner and dinner on Christmas Day. Although, once fed, she would be anxious to head out, regardless of the weather. Nothing compares to an early morning walk on Nantucket, in any weather.

Although she planned to open up the house as soon as she could do her business with Attorney Macy, she knew that it would take at least twenty-four hours to bring the heat up in the old house to habitable temperatures. If she decided to keep the house, not that this was a seriously entertained proposition, she'd most definitely have to replace the ancient, clunky, insufficient furnace in the old stone cellar.

Christmas and the months of January and February meant no waiting in lines for restaurant seating, even though most restaurants close until spring. Fewer people, fewer choices, just the diehards like the Coffin House, The Brotherhood, The Even Keel and the Atlantic Café. Tourists *and* year-rounders are scarce after the first of the year. Most people who stay in their homes to enjoy the quieter autumn season, often through Christmas have, by the first of the year, taken off for warmer climes.

Eating out would be better than getting in groceries for just a few days. She wondered if someone had cleaned out the refrigerator after Bessie died. The funeral had been in Forest Hills Cemetery in Newton in the family plot so Nora had not been to the house since then. Funny thought, she told herself. A clean refrigerator was always a concern of Aunt Bessie whose sister Eloise's fridge, according to Bessie, looked like a scientific experiment in growing mold.

For some reason, because Bessie had never mentioned that the house would be hers, she supposed that it would be left to the Nantucket Historical Society to become a public museum of some kind. Its history, being one of the oldest houses on the island, having been built by a whaling captain named Clarence Starbuck, was mentioned in island chronicles and was always included in the Garden Club spring tour and the Historical Society's fall tour of old homes. She had not expected it would be hers but her aunt had left it and all of her money, not a fortune but a nice sum, to her only niece, after all.

As soon as the word got around, as words do so quickly in such a small and insulated place, the Historical Society communicated with Nora to let her know that, should she choose to sell, they would like to be granted first refusal. The Starbuck name and fame, connected to the Age of Whaling, guaranteed a high value on the old house. In its heyday, when the whaling industry made Nantucket the second wealthiest town in the country until New Bedford stole its glory, houses were being built as fast as they could be raised. What had been little more than an outpost of self-sufficient island families surviving on fishing and small family farms, quickly became become a fashionable, architecturally elegant place. The wealthy whaling captains built homes for their families that were showplaces. Today, they were valuable pieces of history.

She had one last glimpse of the perfect family from the ferry as they were greeted by a handsome, older couple, probably grandparents, awaiting them on the wharf. After a round of many hugs and greetings, they were whisked into a black Tahoe SUV and off they went. Nora wondered where their house was and what their Christmas would be like. She must stop trying to live in other people's lives, she reminded herself. She needed one of her own but she had no damned idea of how to get one. She had a great job in Boston running an art gallery. She had many wonderful friends and she'd had the occasional romance. However, she had not yet met a man she would trust enough to make a life with him; certainly not her latest ex-boyfriend…the jerk. She liked referring to him as a jerk but he had been far more lethal than that. After all, he'd stripped her bank account and taken off with her heart. She could mend that organ, in time, but rebuilding her bank account would take time and restraint. So much for the great new couch in the Home and Hearth catalog and the striped rugs from Dash and Albert. Well, at least she still had her job and now, whatever money had been left her would enable her to spend a few weekends, maybe even her three-week summer vacation on the island if the house took a while to sell.

She had to stop trying to slip into the lives of others. She understood the hollow quality of living in a dream world rather than making the effort to create a reality of one's own. She often asked herself whether it was simple laziness or more like neurotic caution. She wasn't sure she wanted an answer to that query.

By the time the wharf was totally empty, but for a small black and white dog which had taken it upon himself to chaperone her, she started to walk to the inn. She refused two taxis, preferring the short walk up Broad Street. Checking in, Nora was told that Christmas Eve dinner in the dining room would be in two seatings: six o'clock and seven o'clock. She made her choice and headed up the stairs.

The inn was obviously booked solid. The friendly woman at the check-in desk told her what she already knew. "We are so honored that families come back every year, have for decades. New family members are always a pleasure to meet. We have lots of toddler and babies this year. The Winslows from Philadelphia are celebrating their sixty-second anniversary this weekend and their sixty-second Christmas here. They came here on their honeymoon just two days before Christmas in 1943 and Mr. Winslow left for war right after they got back home that year. Imagine that."

Nora could imagine that...for others. She wished she could know such enduring happiness but she was, at almost thirty-one, already too old to make it to a sixty-second wedding anniversary, she told herself. *Good for the Winslows.*

At four in the afternoon, Nora sat re-reading a book from the bookcase in her room, *Green Dolphin Street*, a favorite in her teens. She had chosen the seven o'clock seating for the holiday eve meal. A gentle knock on the door called her from her the wonderful world created by Elizabeth Goudge in the 1940's, to find, standing outside her door, a very nice young man in white shirt and black trousers carrying a large Nantucket Lightship basket full of little, five-inch boxes wrapped in gilt paper tied with red ribbon.

"Merry Christmas, thanks for joining us for the holiday. A gift from the innkeepers."

Nora accepted the little box and thanked the man. As she was closing the door, she spotted the handsome family from the ferry. So much for the family home decorated in anticipation of their arrival. However, that did not keep her from continuing her little fantasy. *The couple met while working on the island one summer, had their engagement party here at the inn and then married in the great room. Every year they return. Now they come with their adorable daughters.*

Get a grip, Nora. Or else start writing romance novels!

She closed the door, although slowly, hopefully inconspicuously, and stood unmoving, thinking about the family that had taken root in her dream life. Was it truly possible for a couple to be utterly happy? Could anyone actually have perfect children, enjoy each other's company, be best friends, love their in-laws, and do fun, interesting things together? Like spend Christmas every year at an inn on Nantucket with all kinds of special effort made to make it magical? She doubted it. Doubting Nora. However, she would love to be proved wrong.

Sticking a postcard provided by the inn, of the inn, into the book as a place mark, Nora washed her face and hands, applied some skin cream, patched her eye makeup and added a coat of lip gloss as protection from the harsh, cold wind. She donned her camel coat and black felt hat and headed down the stairs to the lobby accompanied by strains of Silver Bells. As she descended, she recalled how her aunt had loved seeing her in her camel coat. "Just love how the color accents the caramel streaks in your milk chocolate hair, dear."

Aunt Bessie loved food, both cooking it and eating it. She even loved grocery shopping and woe be to anyone who got her spices out of alphabetical order. She had a charming habit of using food terms as adjectives for everything from Nora's hair to the, "*Aubergine* and apricot sunset over Tuckernuck."

Walking in the brisk air as tiny snowflakes landed on her nose and cheeks, she toted up all the things she loved about the island. Beginning with the time-warp beauty of its stately, old New England homes to street names like, Stone Alley, India Street, Orange Street, Easy Street, Pocomo Road, and Lucretia Mott Lane, she emotionally hugged Nantucket. She loved the cobblestones of Main Street running from the waterfront wharves up the hill, past the water trough that once refreshed horses, to the old Civil War Monument at the apex where Main became Upper Main. Antique shops, bookstores, museums, galleries, restaurants, the ubiquitous t-shirt shops and the up-scale clothing shops where, even on sale, the prices were way above those on the mainland, were all dear to her heart.

Young people quickly learned that, unless they could take over a family business, they probably could not make a living there. Not to mention, afford to live there, starting out after college. Later, the lucky ones inherited family homes and fortunes, but by then, they had usually already made their own way in the world. Money begets money, Aunt Bessie used to say.

Nora had to decide what to do with the house and its contents. Her dream of living there permanently was just that, an amorphous dream. Peripherally, she was aware that these pressing decisions shone a light on the larger issue, her life back in Boston. She walked for over an hour, returning red-nosed and infused with energy. Stepping into the great room at the inn where a blazing fire in the huge fireplace snapped and crackled, she had made no decisions, however she felt great. People sat around drinking sherry or eggnog as if it was were their home living room. Each gathering had established a space with invisible walls surrounding them, seemingly unaware of the others.

Christmas Day dinner was a formal affair as had been that of the evening before. Everyone came dressed and the food was scrumptious and bountiful. Nora saw many of the same families who had enjoyed the last evening's meal, although the family from the ferry was nowhere in evidence. Two tables away from her sat a group of eight she guessed to be around her age, except for one man who seemed to be the leader and probably slightly older. Tall, sandy-haired with a craggy but not aged face, rather, a face that had probably spent too much time in the sun, sailing, playing tennis, or maybe golf. He reminded her of her father from a picture taken when her parents became engaged. Although from a raven-haired family of robust "Black Irish," he had been quite fair-haired and slim, unlike his rugged, rugby-playing siblings. His mother, Nora's grandmother, Nanny Bridget, always kidded him that he was a throwback to long ago Vikings who "Ravaged the land planting their fair Nordic seed in fertile Irish soil." The family story said that one of the invaders had ravished a lovely young family "colleen," creating a new gene pool that contributed to Aidan's handsome but uncharacteristic good looks. She laughed when she told him the family history and the connection between him and the invaders. However, she explained, "That is how the wonderful melting pot continues to add interesting new ingredients so that we Irish are not allowed to be one-dimensional racially or culturally. Ah, but our Irish pride insists of course, and by God we are correct, the Irish are the world's best."

Watching the dynamics at the other table, where it was obvious that the sandy-haired, good-looking man was the center of attention with the others revolving around his sun, Nora could feel the radiation. Now and then, there was a round of boisterous laughter. The happy group seemed quite oblivious of the other diners, some of whom looked askance and others envious. Would someone suggest they take their noisy party elsewhere?

All in the noisy party were outdoorsy types, people who sail in summer and ski in winter, all except for one young man whom Nora decided was either suffering from a form of cancer or, perhaps, Aids. He was decidedly frail, not so much in natural body conformation but as if he has been very ill and the flesh had melted from his otherwise sturdy structure. Bald, a pallid complexion and an obvious lack of stamina emanated off the unfortunate young man. Yet, he held his own, laughing, joking, poking fun but not touching the plate set before him.

Their occasional outbursts were not offensive to Nora but rather, so full of good spirits and general merriment, their bonds of friendship almost palpable, that she wished she could slip over and join them. There would be no sense of loneliness and loss surrounded by such good friends. The kind of friends that are more like close family. She missed Aunt Bessie and dreaded the weighty decisions she would have to face after the holiday.

The sandy-haired man caught Nora looking at him. Looking quickly away, she blushed, surprising herself. Giving her full attention to the delicious ginger crème brulé, she did not see him stand and approach her table.

Stirring sugar into the fragrant coffee just set before her, she assumed the presence at her elbow was the waitperson. Looking up, instead, she discovered the man from the fun-filled table.

"Hi, Max Michelson, innkeeper. Well, not this inn. Don't I wish? My place is down on Center Street."

Before Nora could think of a clever reply or even stop her heart from pounding like a jackhammer, he continued. "No one should sit alone on Christmas day, come on over and join us. We are a bit daffy, but harmless." Her voice absent and her heart skipping, she nodded and, as he placed his hand on her elbow and reached for her coffee cup, she found herself being led into the circle of friendly smiles and greetings.

"Rescued a damsel in need of frivolity," said the man who had indeed rescued Nora from her own shadowed thoughts.

She introduced herself and the bald man attempted to pull out her chair, however the move was apparently too difficult. One of the other young men jumped up to help. As he passed, he patted the bald man on the head and leaned down to kiss the same spot. Nora sat. As she did so, she noticed the linen napkin that had fallen from the bald man's lap onto the floor. Picking it up, she handed it to him. That was when she saw the pink plastic hospital bracelet on his left arm.

One by one, going around the circular table, they introduced themselves.

"Hi, Cathy Wentworth, I work at the Atlantic Café, but it's closed for the holidays until the first week in January; first time off since June. I am with my best friends and thinking of what I want to do next with my life. I am career blocked, at present. My buddies here are full of suggestions. Let's see, so far they have proposed, brain surgeon, Hudson River School painter, street cleaner and, oh yes, Max has suggested dictator of a small country." She stuck her tongue out at Max.

"In my defense, Kathy dear, with your organizational skills and control freak tendencies, I just can't think of a more appropriate career."

"Me next. Randall W. Cosgrove III, at your service."

Everyone laughed and the woman sitting next to him cuffed him gently on the cheek saying, "God, he is such a snob. At the inn, the Woodbox Inn that is, he is just Randy the assistant cook. Jeez Randy, no one is impressed by your Boston Brahmin credentials, so give it a rest."

Randall looked crestfallen, pouting for a moment as if terribly hurt, and then, just when the silence seemed awkward and Nora waited for someone to bridge the abyss, he laughed raucously. He retook his seat, and slapping his hands together said, directly to Nora, taking her hand, "Madam, I had thought to impress you because of your rare and exquisite beauty. My friends, if they are really my friends, have chosen to unmask me. Some time, when we are alone, I shall tell you the terrible story of how my wealthy, aristocratic parents ignore me and how love-starved I am. If you are in the market for a *trés, trés* wealthy man of great passion, I lay my gauntlet at your feet." With that, he bowed his head and everyone, including Nora, laughed uproariously.

Next, the lovely, dark haired woman whom Nora had noticed trying to attract Max's attention all evening, spoke. Nora prided herself on good people reading skills, and this woman exuded smoldering love for Max Michelson or she was a monkey's uncle. She introduced herself as Michelle Gray from Providence Rhode Island, student at Johnson and Wales Culinary Arts School.

"I am doing a semester in France beginning in January and this is my going away party combined with Christmas." Looking from Nora to Max, she smiled, but her beautiful dark eyes belied her happiness. Something was obviously missing and Nora almost felt sad for her. It was obvious to Nora that although Max was Michelle's friend, he had no romantic feelings for her anymore than the other females at the table.

On second thought, Nora was not sorry that Michelle was heading for France.

Michael was last, from his wheelchair where he looked tired and pale but obviously determined not to throw cold water on this party of his best friends he said, "Hi, I'm Michael Shane and I have AIDS." His voice cracked but his smile was there, strong and full of resolve.

"Well, old boy, got to get you back home," Max lovingly tied a blue plaid scarf around Michael's neck while Michelle helped him maneuver into his outer jacket. Lastly, they both pulled a black knitted cap down over his baldhead and did not stop until it came down and covered his eyes.

"Hey, inept caregivers, these eyes are my last delivery system for the appreciation of beauty." Pushing the hat up, Michael added, "On second thought, however, God look at the pigsty we've created for poor Hannah our handmaiden. Leave her a nice, fat tip, mateys."

In a group, they all headed for the door. Nora grabbed her purse and accompanied them. The open door let in a burst of frigid air and Nora saw that Michael seemed to shrink to half his already diminished size. As they left the dining room, a number of people had bid them Merry Christmas. Nora wondered if they were acquaintances who knew that sweet Michael was probably enjoying his last Christmas.

Max held the door as the others departed. Michelle and Randall all but carried Michael down the front steps to the sidewalk. Ice encrusted the bushes beside the entry way and Nora could see passers-by walking cautiously. Hanging over the festively but so tastefully decorated town was a full moon, adding even more silver to the tiny white lights on trees along every sidewalk. Nora waved and called Merry Christmas as the group burst into Silent Night walking as a group down Broad Street. It had turned out to be a wonderful day, despite her concerns...and the absence of Aunt Bessie.

Back in her room, Nora reminded herself that she did not believe in love at first sight. *In fact, woman, didn't you just a few days ago make a decision that you were washing your hands of all that foolishness disguised as so-called romance?* She added, *men stink and even the ones as handsome and funny and clever and seemingly wonderful as Max Michelson soon show their bad boy side. Guaranteed.*

How come then, she wondered, had Max Michelson made her knees go a little wiggly?

She knew the type only too well. Handsome, not in a pretty boy way, but rugged, outdoorsy, a man for all seasons, was Max the innkeeper. His great sense of humor and hale fellow well-met personality would make him the object of pursuit for every female for miles around.

She knew Bessie would immediately like Max. Maybe she even knew, *had known*, him. She wondered how long he'd been an island innkeeper. *Well, forget him, Nora, stay your course. Serious business for the next few days, and then...who knows?*

She slept fitfully that night. Attorney Macy called just after eight in the morning to ask if they could reschedule their appointment for later in the day. That was fine with Nora as she rolled over and slipped back to sleep.

At ten, she showered and dressed in a long corduroy rust-colored skirt and black turtleneck sweater. She added a gold chain and a luggage tan, wide belt. Slipping into her new cozy fur-lined L. L. Bean leather boots, she felt ready to face the day. A pile of Belgian waffles topped with cranberry maple syrup and two cups of coffee later, she headed out to check on the weather.

She hadn't looked to her left into the reception desk foyer as she approached the huge front door, so when she felt someone close behind her and saw the strong hand reach for the knob, she flinched.

"Sorry, did I frighten you, Nora? Hey, we natives are all very friendly here; no need to worry."

His smile, as Nora turned to face him, looked as honest and endearing as Santa Claus. *Damn those weak knees.*

"Good morning, Max. Happy Boxing Day."

He laughed. "Yes, I would expect an old-fashioned girl, sorry, woman, to know that holiday. I bet you read British mysteries. Have you plans for all the Twelve Days of Christmas, as well?"

His tone wasn't mocking, although someone else might have sounded so with those words. "It's icy this morning. Be careful on the steps." With that, Max took Nora's arm and proceeded to guide her down to the sidewalk past the greenery entwined with silver ribbons, tiny silver bells and silver tipped pinecones festooning the wrought iron stair railing.

Before she could think of clever quip he said, "Fair lady, if you have the time I wonder if you might like to see my inn."

The wind chose that moment to gust and cause little white whirlpools of snow to eddy around them. "Unless of course, you have someone waiting for you to open some fabulously expensive gift and sit down to roast goose. As I have neither beckoning me, I would ask your indulgence and let me ply you with my excellent rum eggnog."

Nora laughed and allowed him to take her gloved hand in his. They walked a block up Center Street to his handsome, four-story, white, clapboarded inn. Stopping on the sidewalk, he pointed out the decorating skills of his manager, Melanctha. The front porch railings were covered in ivy, holly and fake sunflowers, wound in and out so that not much of the railing or posts were visible. Like a green, red and gold hedge, an amalgamation of winter and summer, it called out for an explanation of its decorator's intentions.

"Nice touch the sunflowers."

"I know. They are my favorite flowers, planted them all over the yard. Miss them, you know, just needed to add a little hopefulness that spring and summer will come again, soon. Melanctha shares my love of the huge sunny faces."

So, there was a woman in his life. *Cad.* No matter, she'd play along.

"I love summer; it has always been my favorite season as well. I like it, very…original. Melanctha? Like Gertrude Stein's character?"

"Yep, her mother was a real serious Stein fan."

For the next two hours, Max and Nora sat by a blazing fire in the room on the front of the inn used by visitors for reading, playing cards and board games and just chatting. The room exuded charm and welcome. Nora wondered if the clever and original Melanctha's touch had been dominant there as well.

The eggnog was excellent as were the star shaped anise-flavored German Christmas cookies Max called "springerlies." When he brought out date and nut bread sliced thickly and spread with cream cheese, Nora really began to worry that she was intruding on another woman's territory.

"How do you like my cooking, Nora? Learned it at my grandfather's knee. Actually, all the men in our family, back to Lars the Magnificent, who cooked for the Polish king of Sweden, were good cooks.

A handsome, charming, funny, kind and considerate man, who also cooked! No, not possible. *I am suffering from a quick-onset fever that produces hallucination and a fugue state.* Nora's mind raced. Therefore, maybe the unusually named Melanctha was not fully in charge of all things great and beautiful at the inn.

Glancing at the handsome face of the antique grandfather's clock just over Max's shoulder as they sat in the window seat, "Better to view the *madding* crowd," Max had said as he led her to a deeply cushioned window seat, she saw that she had ten minutes to get to Attorney Macy's office.

As she hurried into her boots and coat, pulled the wool hat from her pocket despite what it would do to her hair, and prepared to leave, Max grabbed his car keys and offered a ride.

"Thanks but its only down on Straight Wharf, I can walk it in six minutes."

"Wouldn't think of letting you go without extending the visit every minute I can, Nora the lovely."

Sure, bet you say that to all the women you lure to your charming inn, Max Michelson.

Not seeing the strategically placed mistletoe over the front door, Nora froze when he leaned down to place a brotherly kiss on her lips.

The welcome blast of cold air, as Max pulled open the door, only slightly cooled the rising heat that Nora acknowledged…and fought against.

Reminding herself, once again, that she was a sensible, professional woman newly minted with the power to resist the wiles of handsome, charming men so as not to be stung again, she headed down the steps. This time, she refused Max's hand. She needed the space from him. Just because she found Max Michelson irresistible, did not mean that she had to cave in.

"Do you always drive around in winter in this open jeep, Max?"

"Yup. Love weather. I prefer summer but still, I like to live in the moment. Anyway, the farthest I drive is to the A&P for groceries and the ferry landing to pick up guests. After a winter ferry ride, they get a kick out of the open car. Naturally, I wouldn't do it to them if the inn was in Sconset." He laughed and the temporary pressure brought on by the errant mistletoe was relieved.

Max dropped her off in front of the wonderful old brick former Macy warehouse built in the whaling days, when the Macys were a prominent shipbuilding and whaling family. She'd felt badly when the Artists Association of Nantucket had failed to jump on the chance to purchase the building for its offices and gallery when it was offered a few years back. However, another gallery had opened on the street floor and Attorney William Macy, great, great grandson of the original owner, had set up his law office upstairs.

Nora stood in the bracing air as Max drove off waving up over his head from the open Jeep. She took stock before entering the huge double door decorated in what she had learned as a child were the inspiration for the expression, *dead as a doornail*. The guide at the oldest house on the island had explained that the carpenters who built thick, weather-proof doors (before the advent of storm doors) had doubled up the layers of wood and joined them with long, handmade nails that stuck out the other side about a half inch. When all nails were in place, they hammered the protruding ends down to "deaden" them. They would never pull out after that stabilizing effect.

As she stood there, watching families passing by, it hit Nora that she had no more family, no boyfriend, no husband, and no children. It also occurred to her that she could, if she let herself, fall apart and cry until her heart physically ached. And then, what? No, she had to stay the course and, as her childhood sailing instructor at the Nantucket Yacht Club had taught her, *set your sail, point your bow and go for it.* She had no other choice.

TWO

Attorney Bill Macy's office, on the second floor of the old warehouse, looked more like a history museum than a law office. The interior brick walls had never been covered and, over the centuries, they had developed a lovely patina. Bill kept the old woodstove that once provided his ancestor and his staff with comfort as they checked ships' *ladens* or *burdens* as they were also called.

The brick warehouse on Straight Wharf had also been one of thirty factories, from large to tiny, back-room household businesses producing whale oil candles. Nora looked around as the attorney sifted through a manila folder on the enormous mahogany desk that separated them.

"You certainly have a wonderful collection of Americana here, William."

"Started collecting as a kid. My friends thought I was what kids today would call a "geek," because I was so interested in the island's history of whaling. My family was prominent in the whaling industry. I got hooked early; by the time I was ten, I knew more about whales and whaling in the Pacific Ocean than my pals did about sports or cowboy movies."

Nora smiled. She liked it when she met someone as in love with the island as she was. "The Whaling Museum must be envious. They would probably love to get their hands on all of this."

Bill smiled. "I can see you love this stuff too, Nora. Well, you will be happy to know that it all goes to the Nantucket Whaling Museum upon my death. Although I plan to live a very long life, it's in my good genes, so they will just have to wait and salivate."

Nora liked the man immediately.

The attorney gave her a look of apology as he took a phone call. She looked around at the magnificent whalebone scrimshaw art in the form of brooches, sewing needles, yarn winders, tiny chests and other magnificent things down to commonplace clothespins. She knew that all that beauty was attributed to bored sailors who made gifts for loved ones at home. Recalling her father's definition of sailing, "Hours and hours of tedium interspersed with moments of stark terror," she understood what inspired such creations.

Phone call taken care of, the attorney turned his attention to the pile of papers waiting for Nora's signature. She felt like she was re-taking SATs, there was so much that had to be covered legally, in order for her to take possession of Aunt Bessie's house.

Not only the old family home on Main Street had been left to her, but also the "shack" out on Coatue, the sandy outer beach that protected the inner harbor from the sometimes-feisty Atlantic. Aunt Bessie and Nora had always spent a few weeks out there every summer...such a difference from the antique-filled home in town. There, they swept out the cottage once a week, only when the underfoot crunching became annoying. They read by oil lamp, cooked on a hibachi and slept pretty much on the same schedule as the sun. Many happy hours had been spent in nothing but a bathing suit, roaming the dunes, hiking out to the lighthouse at Great Point and lying in her room gazing out the leaky skylight at the full moon. Aunt Bessie always planned their stay around the time of the full moon. Clever lady.

Going through the lists of the big house's contents seemed to Nora to be so clinical. She had grown up among the antiques in Aunt Bessie's house on Main Street. They were just there, as if they and the house had morphed into existence together one day, way back in the days of whaling. Not that she did not appreciate them; her aunt taught her what she knew of their provenance and the craftspeople who had created them. When Nora was on the island, she existed in a kind of on-going history lesson sprinkled with bits of island gossip.

Bill Macy seemed to read Nora's mind when they broke for tea delivered by the attorney's secretary. "Nora, do not let yourself be rushed. Certainly, I do not mean to cause you to feel that you must make immediate decisions about the properties. Take your time. Mistakes occur when we rush. This is too big a proposition that could end up with you regretting things later, if you rush it."

It was then that Nora realized that that was exactly what had been troubling her most since the attorney called to tell her that Aunt Bessie had left her everything. It would be so easy just to hang onto both properties and all the wonderful furnishings, and just coast.

"You do not have to do anything until you are absolutely ready to make decisions. In fact, why not go home to Boston and come back in the good weather. Of course, I do not know how much time you can reasonably take from your job, but it will all be here, waiting for you, whenever you feel ready.

"Thanks Mr. Macy, for the advice. It is a bit, as kids say today, awesome. I feel as if a mountain is threatening to fall on me or an enormous wave headed right for me and I have no idea of how to avoid it. I love the old place but I know I cannot afford to take it on and live here. What would I do for work? I couldn't even afford the upkeep on the house on an island salary, let alone continue to eat and pay the utilities."

"Nora, you are creating problems that are not there." The man smiled, Nora noted, like a wily fox about to spring on an unwary rabbit.

"Did you really think that your dear aunt left you cash poor and property rich? Dear lady, your aunt was a very wealthy woman and now...so are you."

Nora sat stunned. What *had* she been thinking? Did she look as overwhelmed as she felt? Attorney Macy, like a mirror reflecting her stunned image, smiled at her kindly. "Dear Nora, there are funds in the account set aside to have a caretaker on duty overseeing things when you are not here. Your aunt had 'no flies' on her, as they say. She knew you would hesitate to leave your busy life and fine career in Boston to hide out here in the off-season. Everything has been arranged. Naturally, as the new owner, you can make any changes you like. However, know this, the money left to you will allow you to keep everything in stasis until you are ready to make further decisions. Whether to keep the properties for summer occupation only or come here to settle permanently, whatever else you might choose to do is quite up to your choice and personal discretion. I would however suggest you do not choose to rent the house in town. Perhaps the Coatue cottage, but the house has too many valuable things in it to trust to renters."

In the days that followed, Nora, having extended her leave from her job so that she would not feel rushed in making her decisions, found that, despite her newfound wealth, she still felt overwhelmed. Walking back to the old house that she'd opened up and settled into once the central heating had been checked and found to be fine, she thought about going to visit Max at his inn. She could use a friend to talk things out with, and although she had a good friend in Boston who'd listen and understand, for some reason, Max came to mind. She corrected herself and instead of turning right on Center Street, she continued on up Main Street.

She had been approached by no less than six island antique dealers who'd inquired as to whether she wanted to sell the entire houseful of antiques, rugs, paintings, old maps, first edition books etc. A letter had arrived from Monaco, France, from a man who knew her aunt and knew that she had passed away. He offered his condolences followed by an offer to buy the house for a figure that choked Nora.

She opened the letter with the surprising Monaco postmark right in the post office. "Curious as a cat, my Nora" he aunt had often said. Reading the astoundingly large offer, she laughed aloud. The clerks and other patrons smiled in response to the amused woman among them.

Slipping the letter into her fleece coat jacket, Nora slid out the front door onto Federal Street. People walking dogs and children with rosy noses and mittened hands passed by enjoying the cold but sunny day. She headed for the Even Keel to meet Bill Macy for coffee. He had become a good, reliable friend and confidante. Funny, she thought, as she headed the half block to Main Street, although she liked talking to Bill and relied on him for good guidance, she was not attracted to the man. She knew that he was single and he was an attractive man, no doubt about that, but the chemistry was not there. Unfortunately, she suspected that the chemistry was working for him in that regard.

Over cappuccinos and raspberry cream cheese Danish, she showed the Monaco letter to Bill. "Wow, you could really be a wealthy woman with that in your bank account. Are you tempted, Nora?" He put his hand on hers and left it there. She would have to find a way to let him know that she did not share his growing feelings for her. Damn, she didn't want to lose his friendship, but she was neither ready for starting something deeper nor wanted that with him.

"I'm heading out to Sconset today to check on a friend's property. There was some damage done there, probably by kids, and the owner wants me to take a look. We could take a look at the Moors, always pretty covered in a little light snow, and swing around to Sankaty Light. I like seeing these places when they seem to be sleeping, undisturbed by tourists. Are you interested, Nora?"

Bill Macy was so easy to be with and she was certainly appreciative of his sage, low-key guidance. However, better not to encourage him, at least until she was more sure of her footing. Not that she expected to fall in love with him, but stranger things had happened. He would make a great husband and father. Not that she was ready, nor anxious, to join the ranks of her married friends with children.

"I'd love to any other time, Bill, but my boss has set up a conference call with a client in Italy interested in two of our very costly paintings. My boss is the business guy, and I am the art expert. Not to brag, but compared to what my boss knows about fine art, despite his owning four galleries, I am invaluable to his very existence in the business."

"I hope he appreciates that, Nora. Your job sounds fascinating and absorbing. Well, another time, then. Got to go. This was fun. Let's do it again, soon."

The next day, when Bill called to ask her to meet him for lunch at the Brotherhood, she had to accept. He had some more papers for her to sign so he could transfer Aunt Bessie's blue chip stocks into Nora's name.

"So much nicer doing business over lunch and I want you to try the Brotherhood's quahog chowder...the best anywhere. Well, I will let you decide, but I feel confident you will agree with my assessment. How about one o'clock?"

Digging into the steamy, aromatic quahog chowder, so thick the spoon stood up in it, Nora smiled at Bill and nodded. "This is wonderful. I don't remember it being so good before."

"No, it's the new chef. Believe it or not, he is Puerto Rican. He brought his recipe with him. Everyone is loving it."

"How did a Puerto Rican learn to make such outstanding New England clam chowder, Bill?"

Bill laughed as he pushed aside his empty chowder mug. "His mother was born on Cape Cod. I asked him exactly your question and he told me that his mother went on vacation in the Caribbean, met a man who ran a restaurant in San Juan, they fell in love, and she stayed on there. She brought to his menu not only excellent clam chowder but clam fritters and cranberry pie."

"Great story. I think however that Mama added some really nice Puerto Rican spices to her recipe."

Bill smiled. "You have a fine educated palette, Nora. That is exactly what takes the fine chowder up a notch. Secret spices. Jorge has sent to him from home. His brother runs a place called "The Spice Necklace." He imports spices from all the Caribbean Islands and he sells women beautiful necklaces with spices strung on strong string. I will have Jorge order one for me to you."

Nora smiled and thanked him, unable to find a polite way to let him know that his campaign was not going to win her over. Would he continue to want to be friends once she made it clear that romance was not on the agenda for the two of them, she wondered?

As they waited for their next course to come, Nora gazed rather absently around the room. She knew the place well and loved their food, but especially the ambiance. The very low ceiling was original to the space that had been the basement of the building. It was there that they had stored barrels of rum, salt, dried fish and other assorted goods necessary to the inn that had been located upstairs.

As Nora's eyes passed over the other diners, the people sitting at the bar and the busy wait staff, they stopped at a table over in the shadows. Her heart skipped a beat as she spotted a familiar face. Max Michelson sat alone at a table for eight. Obviously, he was waiting for his jolly entourage.

Just then, the door opened and in they tumbled. Although Michael was not with them, and there was no sign of the smitten Michelle (wasn't she going off to some place, right after Christmas?), the rest of the gang was there. Shaking off the snow that had begun falling softly as Nora and Bill sat eating, just by being there Max's friends shone a bright light into the corner where Max was waiting. Standing to welcome them, Max said something that got them all laughing uproariously. A funny joke, Nora thought, watching his delivery. Body language. Nice body, she thought, catching herself in time to avoid being seen by Max. She quickly turned back to Bill who was obviously basking in the light of good friends shining across the room. What if Max turned out to be just a great party boy who thrived on having an audience, but who steered clear of real relationships? That would be just her luck.

Bill's voice came to her mid-consideration of Max the innkeeper's real personality and motives. "Good old Max. Always the center of good times."

Hoping her voice sounded only mildly interested, simply making town connections, she asked, "Do you know Max Michelson?"

"Everyone knows good old Max. He's a very popular guy on the island. Always enjoying himself. To see him with his friends, you'd think he hadn't a trouble in the world. Some people just have a knack for shedding the problems of their lives for a few hours to have fun. Have you met him, Nora?"

"Yes," Nora paused. "Yes, we met on Christmas Day at the Jared Coffin House holiday dinner. He was with the same group, plus a man named Michael who has AIDS." Remembering the sweet, bald, and obviously very weakened man, she wondered if he had been too ill that day to join the gang.

"Max was kind enough to invite me over saying that no one should be alone on Christmas. I am afraid I was feeling a little lonely that day without Aunt Bessie. They cheered me up with their infectious cheeriness."

"Tell me about your holidays with Bessie, Nora."

Nora appreciated Bill's proffered opportunity to concentrate on great memories rather than on the enigmatic Max. Unless Bill could read her mind, he did not know that he had saved her from some sticky thoughts. Their next course, broiled haddock with lobster stuffing for Bill and lobster Newburg for Nora arrived and they dug in while the meal was hot. Not until the dessert, pumpkin cranberry pie, disappeared off their plates and coffee was served, did they return to the subject of Nora's Christmas memories.

My holidays with Aunt Bessie were always such fun. Many of her old friends gave Christmas Eve parties, so she felt no need to give one herself. We kind of moved around town like a two-headed snake looking for nourishment. We walked from house to house, eating, drinking; Aunt Bessie was a teetotaler and I, of course, drank the children's punch, and singing carols. I arrived from school a few days before and we did our gift shopping together. She always waited for me to arrive although it was usually slim pickings in the shops by then. When my parents died, although the Woodmans were so good, taking me in and treating as if I was their own child, I don't think I'd have survived as well as I did without Aunt Bessie."

"I remember her well. She was an old friend of my mother's. In fact, I bet you don't remember this, you and I made a snowman together one Christmas Eve. Well, not just you and me. There were a bunch of kids there who, when the party got boring, headed out to throw snowballs and construct a snowman with rather a dinosaur look to it. Dinosaurs were all the rage for us boys at that time."

"I do remember." She actually had no recollection of Bill, but the event was still crystal clear.

"Did you know that she made her own special recipe Christmas candies? I helped once I arrived from school, but mostly she did all the work herself ahead of time. As I recall, she began in October…caramels, fondants, peanut butter and pumpkin fudge were among her specialties. And, oh, yes, her chocolate truffles just melted in your mouth like warm butter."

Before she had a chance to sensor her thoughts, the words poured out, "Max and his friends certainly did save the day for me. I was pretty down thinking about Aunt Bessie but they cheered me up."

Can you manage to keep that man's name out of this conversation, Nora? Let alone his face, as it looked, so close to hers under the mistletoe.

Bill didn't seem to mind her mention of the man entertaining his friends across the room. "Max has been here for about fifteen years. Worked for a long time at an inn on lower Center Street. He always worked hard, did just about everything from maintenance to cooking to taking charge of the reservations and front desk. He worked for Miriam Wenton who told everyone how much she depended upon him and how the inn could not possibly run without him. And then, Oh, I probably should not be telling tales out of school, I should let you hear it from him, Nora..."

"Oh, no, I don't expect I shall ever be speaking with him again Bill. After all, I'll be gone soon and I am not part of his in-group of fun loving friends. Tell me, is it a bad story?"

"Well, he was there for many years and I suppose everyone just thought they had something going. You know island gossip. One day however, Miriam just took off traveling around the world. She was single and had plenty of money so she just left Max to run the place. Whatever happened between them, if in fact there was anything beyond an employer/employee relationship, did not elicit from Max the kind of reaction any other man might have exhibited. I mean, she just took off without a by your leave, as the British like to say, leaving Max holding the bag. Or, in this context, the inn."

"When did he leave that inn to go to the one he runs now?"

"He kept Miriam's inn ticking along, making money for her as it always had and then, one day a few years ago, she returned unexpectedly with a new husband. She wasn't in town twenty-four hours before Max was fired with no explanation, as I heard. The new husband took over and in two years the place was bankrupt and Miriam left the island. No one knows what happened to the husband. Wow, I sound like a real gossip, don't I?"

Nora smiled and patted his hand. "Don't worry, I am the soul of discretion." As Bill moved to put his hand on top of Nora's, she pulled hers away. It was an awkward moment.

"Well," Bill continued, "Max always lands on his feet. He moved in with friends but soon he was running another place over on India Street until the new opportunity came along. He seems to be settled in where he is now. Naturally, anyone who knew how capable he is was going to grab him fast. I guess he did fall into some debt for awhile because he got booted from Miriam's inn just about this time of year, when almost everything is closed or planning to right after the New Year."

Nothing ventured, nothing gained, Nora told herself as she slipped the next question at Bill. "So, except for maybe a thwarted relationship with the dragon lady, he's a confirmed bachelor?" Was that casual enough, she wondered?

Bill looked as if her questions about Max Michelson were not where he had been hoping the luncheon would be going, but he was too polite to show any irritation.

"I heard that he used up his savings taking off for a few months to go somewhere in the tropics; although, it might have been Australia…not sure. Nothing like a warm climate and swaying palms to bring a troubled man around to a new perspective."

"But he came back to Nantucket."

"He considers this home. Max is a survivor. As you can see, he loves an audience, people gravitate to him; not that he isn't sincere. He returns friendship in kind. Max Michelson is a decent, capable and dependable comrade. Once in Max's sphere, he will do anything he can for you, should you need time, money, whatever."

Just the answer Nora was looking for…at least one of them.

Bill excused himself to speak to a client at the bar and Nora took the opportunity to pull out her compact to use the mirror for some spying. She giggled to herself, realizing she was acting like a silly schoolgirl with a crush.

Damn, he was looking at her looking at him. Caught. No, think about it, you were checking your makeup and just happened to catch him looking this way. No big deal. She slipped the compact back into her purse.

Bill returned to the table and they prepared to leave. She wished there was a back way out rather than having to pass right by Max's table. What was she doing, she asked herself, acting like a teenager? A quick hello, keep moving and, out the door you go, Nora. *Be a big girl and face a difficult situation with grace and poise.* Aunt Bessie's voice inside Nora's head sounded reassuring.

Then, Max was beside her and she could smell his cologne. She thought it might be Bay Rum; a hint of the tropics, swaying palm trees, and a man on the run from a bad deal. What else happened to him down under or wherever he went for his readjustment therapy, flashed through Nora's mind? Once again, creating a story in her head.

THREE

Extending his hand to Bill, smiling broadly as he told him it was good to see him out and around rather than holed up in his office with his "...stuffy whaling collection," he, at first, ignored Nora. The men laughed and then, Max turned to Nora.

"Nice to see you again Nora, hope we brightened your holiday. Michael says you are the most gorgeous woman he's ever seen. He's developed quite a crush on you. "

"How is Michael doing?" asked Bill, looking concerned.

"Pretty good...At least, no more chemo. He took a stand; says he doesn't want to spend his final days vomiting. He has even gotten some appetite back and we all just take turns making sure he gets out for fresh air and his favorite foods. Lots of ice cream...I bought a new-fangled ice cream maker so I could supply him. Melanctha cleans his place and the ladies at the library keep him supplied with books and videos. What time he has left, his friends intend to make good and loving."

"He's such a sweet man. A lucky man to have all of you caring for him. Does Michael have family, Max"

"Just a sister who lives in Italy. She's arriving tomorrow, in fact. Michael is all excited about seeing her. Well, nice seeing you two."

Max returned to his friends as Bill and Nora walked to the door, stopping to say hello to the gathering, before leaving. Exchanging wishes for a Happy New Year, Nora caught Max looking directly at her. Little nerve endings tingled along her spine. There was no doubt the man confused her. He was certainly inscrutable. A hearty fellow well met and yet, she suspected that he was not adept at one on one relationships. Just a women's intuition thing that, she reminded herself, was not for her to validate. She had not come to the island to get personally involved. *This time, let whatever story coalesces around the man in the depths of your mind remain in the realm of fiction. This man has no place in the factual workings of your real life. End of story.*

The blast of icy air outside the too-warm restaurant was shocking. Nora pulled up her fur-lined hood and reached into her pocket for gloves. They were not there. Surely she had slipped them into her pocket when they arrived. She stopped to check the ground. No, they hadn't fallen. The door opened behind her and Max stepped outside with her gloves in his hand.

"You'll probably be needing these, Nora. I personally love this weather. Something about my Scandinavian blood; don't own a pair of winter gloves." Max looked up at the leaden sky and took a deep breath. Nora quashed the thought that she was meant to read into that something about the man's cold heart.

"Well, got to go. I have an appointment back at the office in about six minutes. Thanks for a lovely visit, Nora. See you tomorrow at the office at about eleven?"

"Yes, thanks for the lunch Bill. Eleven will be just fine. See you then."

Bill walked hastily down Broad Street as Nora stood beside Max feeling awkward and tongue-tied.

"Great guy, isn't he? Best lawyer anyone could have. He handled something for me a few years ago that saved my neck. So, where are you off to Nora?"

"I'll probably check the shops on Center Street and buy some decadent treat at the chocolate shop, then back to the inn and a good book."

"Stay right there, let me grab my jacket and I'll join you." With that he went back in the door and Nora stood fighting the butterflies in her stomach.

Returning wearing a lightweight jacket over his cotton crew neck sweater, India wondered about the hot and cold contradictions the man emanated. She could not shake the feeling that Max's outward appearance as the jester and friend to all covered something dark and chilly inside…maybe a badly broken heart. *Not for me to worry about nor attempt to fathom.*

"Do you have the time for a stroll? I want to show you a place I have my sights on for my own inn. It's not far. Will you be warm enough?"

"Yes, I'm fine. I'd love a stroll. So, you are thinking buying your own place, then?"

"I've always run places for other people. I'm good at it, but what I want is my own place to put my own imprint on. As you know, real estate prices have gone totally out of this hemisphere, therefore making it happen is taking me longer than I had hoped."

At the top of Broad Street, they turned the corner by the Jared Coffin House where Nora was staying, and headed down Center toward Main Street. Every house and shop, and even the post office, was tastefully decorated for the holiday season. They passed couples and families out walking in the cold, crisp air, making crunching sounds on the snow that had turned icy overnight.

They talked little, paying attention to icy places on the sidewalk. Now and then, surprisingly, Max took Nora's elbow like a *gentleman of old,* she noted. Pointing to a large pineapple strategically placed between rosy red apples and green pears sitting on fresh pine branches above a doorway, she asked Max if he knew that the pineapple is the symbol of hospitality.

"Yes, in fact, we have a pineapple on our welcome sign at the inn. It's mostly an old New England tradition, although I don't imagine early Nantucketers had much access to pineapples, particularly at Christmas."

"Bill happened to mention it today. He explained that because so many whaling ships spent time in the Pacific, hunting the valuable sperm whale, the custom was adopted to represent the fortune they reaped from that area of the globe.

Again, they walked along in companionable silence. As they crossed Main Street, Nora looked left toward the harbor delighting in the Dickensonian feel of Christmas on Nantucket that she had known since childhood. She could not imagine being anywhere else at that time of year. If she sold Aunt Bessie's house, her ties to the place she loved more than anywhere else would be severed permanently. As Max had pointed out, only multi-millionaires could afford Nantucket real estate prices these days.

They headed up Orange Street past the impressive austere Unitarian Meeting House, turning just beyond it onto a tiny lane called, Windward Alley. As they approached the handsome, foursquare house painted barn red with white trim, Nora recalled knowing a girl who lived there years ago. She had played with the girl, Samantha, and later, they took sailing lessons together at the yacht club.

"Oh, I've always loved this old house. I knew the family who lived here. Is this the place you want to open as an inn? It is certainly large enough. I always wondered about just one small family, father, mother and one daughter, living in all these rooms. It's perfect."

"Yes, it's for sale but way beyond my budget. However, I am putting together or rather, trying to put together, a consortium of islanders to invest in it and let me run it…just wanted to show you where my dreams lie."

"I hope they come true for you, Max."

"Look up." He pointed. "Up on the widow's walk you have a wonderful overview of the harbor. I'm told by Mabel at the library that when the house was originally built for a member of the Starbuck family, there were no houses in front of it and you could see the water from the first floor."

"Yes, the building boom on the island in the years when whaling made this place one of the most prosperous places in the country, really changed it, I've read."

"Yup, until New Bedford stole the industry from the island, this was the third wealthiest city in the country."

"I love the history of our island. How many rooms would you have to rent out?"

"Five more than I have now. In fact, if you have the time, come back to my inn and let me show you the redecorating I've done upstairs. The owners trusted me to honor the integrity of the house's age and to keep it authentic. It was fun spending someone else's money doing something I really enjoy. You have seen only the downstairs. The upstairs is very nautical with great wallpapers I found in New York, lots of blue and white and touches of red and yellow. I found great striped rugs at Dash and Albert and added some antiques from local shops. The combination really works."

Hmm, she noted, *my favorite color scheme.*

"Unless you'd rather get back to that good book."

What the heck, the book could wait. In fact, in this man's company, Nora could imagine letting everything of importance wait. She set aside her theories about him, hoping that if she just relaxed and let their new friendship find its own natural course, it would sail a straight tack.

The tour of the second and third floors of the inn, complete with details of where Max had found each decorating piece, how he'd chosen each paint color and why, was fun. The sunny day turned to dusk as they sat in the front room drinking hot chocolate and eating the most delicious Madeleine's Nora had ever tasted.

"You will have to come back in the daytime to see the garden." Nora turned toward the window but all she could see were long, needle-like icicles hanging from the top of the window frame, and their reflections.

"I have a male and a female holly so, lots of nice, red berries. In summer there are huge, eight foot tall sunflowers and black-eyed susans, zinnias and lots and lots of herbs, and four varieties of tomatoes."

"You must love to garden."

"Yes, I'm pretty much a homebody. I love being with the guests but I know that I could also be a hermit. Just give me an acre of friable land, a library full of books and I would stop shaving, live in a bathing suit and vegetate. But, tell me about you. I've been monopolizing the conversation about me and my dreams. You run an art gallery in Boston and you've recently inherited your aunt's house. Full stop. That is all I know."

"Well, that's pretty much it. I am so busy all day at the gallery that I, too, am happy to go home to cook my dinner and then sit reading until bedtime. I guess I am a homebody, too. I have friends, although I prefer not to keep up with their frenetic pace. Nightclubbing and such just isn't for me. I spent all my childhood and through college years here in the summer with my Aunt Bessie...who died recently. Bill Macy was her lawyer or his father was until he died last year and Bill took over. She left me her house and a tiny cottage out at 'Sconset, and I have to decide what to do with them."

"In a perfect world what would you choose to do?"

"Oh, that's easy. In a perfect world where I could live anywhere and do anything?"

"Yup. Spill your guts out, Nora Kavanagh."

She recalled Attorney Macy's words that she could survive on the money she'd inherited if she lived a quiet life. Was that so unlikely a plan? Finding work on the island would be slim and not equal to her curriculum vitae. She could clerk in a shop or waitress, but probably not find work running a gallery. Those nice positions were cemented in place already.

"Well, I'd keep the house, make some necessary improvements, like a better furnace, a new hot water heater, and a new kitchen stove. Other than that, the house is absolutely perfect. I love Aunt Bessie's house. However, it is very old and would probably, over time, eat up every cent I could come up with, just maintaining it."

"Okay, continuing on with the dream. No holds barred. What would you do for yourself? A new career? Volunteer as docent at the Whaling Museum? Work for charities, what for Nora?

"Well. Let's see. I guess I'd open a gallery on Main Street with all the other galleries and do a retrospective of all the great artists who ever came here to paint, over the years. I know that the Artists Association of Nantucket has managed to accumulate a great collection of work from early island painters. They don't have the space to put it on permanent display. My idea would be to combine retrospectives with new work from island painters."

Just then, the kitchen door swung wide open and there stood the most gorgeous caramel skinned woman Nora had ever set her eyes on. Ebony black hair pulled tightly back to frame her perfect face, and heavy turquoise jewelry at her ears, throat and climbing up both arms, gave her the appearance of a latter day Nefertiti.

"Max you *haunt*, you revenant, I thought to find you gone when I returned. Gone to Fiji or Pitcairn Island on a sailing ship. Joined a pirate crew, perhaps. A sight for sore eyes."

Max laughed and rose to go to the woman. Enveloping her in a bear hug as he spun her around with her feet off the floor, she shouted at him like a banshee. "Crazy man, you put me down or I tear out your thinning hair and blacken both your eyes."

"Nora, this is Melanctha, my assistant, without whom the house would fall into anarchy. Although, she *has* been missing for six weeks. "

"Like Gertrude Stein's Melanctha?"

"Yes, my mother was a great reader." She put out her hand toward Nora, and she took it. Her hand was soft and warm and felt like friendship. "So pleased to meet you Miss Nora, but in fact, it is the master who makes it all work. I am but a cog in a wheel."

As she leaned close, as if sharing a private secret, Nora could see that she was not as young as Nora at first thought. Close up, her lovely face showed lines around her eyes and telltale vertical lines above her upper lip. There were silver streaks at her temples, details that only made her more attractive and exotic.

Melanctha's fragrance filled the air like a tropical breeze.

"I yearn for my pillow; it has been a very long day. The grandchildren, they wear me down. The flight was bumpy and the captain surly. So, I will say goodnight and Merry Christmas, Happy New Year to you both."

Max kissed her cheek and off she went. When she reached the doorway to the front hall, she turned. "Your energy is flagging, Nora. But all will be well, follow your heart."

"Melanctha cared for my mother when she was ill and dying in Jamaica years ago. She is an amazing woman. She sees things in auras or something, I've never asked for a full explanation. She is never wrong, I can tell you that. When she lost her husband and I was just starting out here, she needed a new purpose. She came and ever since then, wherever I go, from inn to inn, she is there to help me. She is a whiz with numbers, personable with guests, a great cook, and of course, never fails to check me when I'm spinning out of control. She's been back in Jamaica for six weeks with her children and grandchildren. She lost her son in October and needed to be back there with family."

Finally, it seemed to Nora that she should leave. People staying at the inn had begun returning from their day's activities. Max went to greet each of them warmly and answer questions, like what restaurants were open for dinner.

Max offered to walk Nora back to the Jared Coffin House and she refused. "Stay here where it is toasty warm, I'll be fine."

At the door, Max leaned down and kissed her cheek, calling her attention to the mistletoe above her head. They laughed and Nora quickly stepped out into the cold.

Lying in the canopied bed, strains of piped-in Christmas Carols coming up the stairs from the great room at the bottom of the stairs, Nora reminded herself that she had more urgent things to attend to than analyzing Max Michelson. They lived in different worlds and hers would soon be calling her back to Boston. End of story.

FOUR

For the next few days, Nora spent hours walking through the old house searching for answers. She needed Aunt Bessie's wisdom, but all she had were memories of wonderful times spent there with her aunt in the house built by her sea captain ancestor to house his large family. Should she keep the house or sell? Give up her life and her job in Boston and move to Nantucket permanently? Would that be pure folly? She supposed that, since Aunt Bessie had left her the house rather than bequeathing it to the Nantucket Historical Association, she meant Nora to keep it.

Bessie's love for the house went bone deep, therefore, to sell it would be a betrayal of that love, right? Nora went round and round, always ending up in the same place. Questioning the sanity of giving up a great job in Boston for the uncertainty of living in a seasonal place hanging onto a house that would always demand costly upkeep, and that was just the beginning. She would be leaving her friends behind, choosing to live an almost cloistered life thirty miles off shore. Round and round she went, confused and troubled, although she always came back to her love of the old house that she shared with her aunt.

It did not escape her however, that, if she had not met Max Michelson, her perspective might be different. Try as she might, she could not push away the thought that if she lived on the island, he and she might build something together. Unless, of course, she was reading the man wrong and he was only being polite and friendly toward her because it came naturally to him. Certainly, his habit of focusing his full attention on whomever he was with had made him successful as an innkeeper. Was she just another conquest of his bottomless charm?

Her pragmatic side warned her that her heart could lead her to make an enormously foolish decision. It even occurred to her that she might sell the big house in town and live out in the cottage at Sconset to save money, until the full reality struck. Winter way out there with all the summer houses closed up and only a small local convenience grocery store sounded a bit austere, however. She didn't even know if the house had heat.

She remained at the inn rather than move into the house, because all the systems had been shut down by the caretaker after Bessie died. Turning on the water and heat for just few days would be foolish. Her sleep was troubled with doubts and conflicting plans. Awakening abruptly from a deep sleep, the bedside clock told her it was four-twenty, and the sound coming from outside was icy snow falling. She pulled the covers up over her head and tried to push intruding thoughts and pending decisions away. She knew better than to fall into the dead of night trap waiting to torture the mind with scary thoughts and troubling scenarios…the worst time to think about one's troubles.

The next thing she knew, it was eight-thirty and the sun was shining in through the frosty windows of her room. Long icicles decorated the top of the tall window and she could hear children outside, shouting and probably tossing icy snowballs.

The long hot shower helped to wash away some of the anxiety over her nocturnal debate. It had always been Aunt Bessie who helped her to find her way through the personal mazes and conundrums that required a level head. She had helped her choose what colleges she should apply to and which car to buy for her very first as well as which job being offered had the best prospect for not only advancement but, personal satisfaction.

What she needed was a good breakfast. Preparing to go down to the dining room, thinking of ordering the quintessential Nantucket breakfast of broiled haddock, baked beans, home fries, and cranberry bread, her cell rang. It was her boss from the gallery on Newbury Street.

"I really need you Nora, the place is falling apart. I just do not know what to do with the new stuff that's piling up. Marilyn Swift is on my neck hourly. She wants us to show her client's work, a one-woman show is what she's demanding but we've promised the place to the Beacon Hill Art Association members for the dates she wants. I just don't know how you juggle it all and come out clean. Can you come back soon? Please."

She gave him the answer he wanted, if fairly ambiguous, "Just and soon as I can."

After a hearty breakfast, she put on boots, coat, hat, scarf and gloves and headed down Main Street toward Straight Wharf. The streets were as busy and bustling as a summer day. Bill was just coming out the front door of his building and greeted her with a big smile. "Let's walk. We can talk about things while we breathe in fresh air."

As they headed up cobblestoned Main Street, she shared her immediate problem. "I guess I have to return to Boston. My boss is not happy. He hates being at the gallery. I don't know what I am going to do about Viburnum Gate. It is all too overwhelming."

"When your aunt named the house for the viburnum bush at the moongate, according to my father, she was in love with an artist. I believe he did a painting of the house, although I've never seen it. Up until then, the house was simply known as the Captain's House. Not exactly unique since nearly all the fine houses of that period were built by whaling captains."

"Aha, so Aunt Bessie was in love with an artist. Oh, I wish I had the painting."

"How about coming with me to see the new exhibit at the Whaling Museum? I lent them my great-grandfather's magnificent collection of scrimshaw. I think you will like it."

Two hours later, having enjoyed her time with Bill, she stepped in through the front door of Aunt Bessie's house. *My house,* she said to herself although it sounded quite strange. The house was frigid. Ice had formed on the inside of the windows which she was sure was not a good thing. If she kept the house she would naturally want to correct all the things that undermined the good health of the old place. It was hardly a project she could take on without having a lot of free money. Sure, Aunt Bessie had left her a bit of money but not enough to make things right in the beloved house. Better to sell it to someone with the wherewithal to do the job right. For the sake of the house.

She could see her aunt walking through the house, a terry dishcloth thrown over her shoulder, as she always did when working in the kitchen, announcing plans for their day. Nora walked through the cold, empty, echoing rooms waiting. Although she could not identify what it was that she was waiting for. She felt an emptiness inside her that ached like a toothache.

She locked the front door and headed back to the Jared Coffin House, resolved to put off the decision until spring. Packing up her duffel bag and laptop case, she felt as if she had, at least, set a goal for herself. She still had a great many decisions to make but the house would wait for her final decision as it had waited for centuries. She headed for Steamship Wharf and the ferry.

Two and half hours later, she stood on the doorstep of the only other person she could depend on for helping her to make wise decisions.

"Well if it isn't the new heiress and mistress of Viburnum Gate on my doorstep." Marsha hugged her tightly and led her into her warm, inviting cook's kitchen recently added to the two-hundred-year old house in the historic village of Cummaquid on Cape Cod.

She served Nora a hot cup of raspberry spice tea that she mixed up herself from her huge garden of fruits, vegetables, herbs and exotic plants. Marsha's home business, in one of the property's old barns, Magic Potions by Marsha, featured natural teas and tisanes, dried herb mixtures for cooking and medicinal purposes, bunches of herbs for hanging "to bring about certain results." She had given Nora a huge bunch of lavender to hang by her bed when she was having trouble sleeping during a stressful period at work. Marsha called herself a modern day witch/alchemist but to Nora she was a rock and a safe harbor whenever she needed the same.

Marsha was Nora's best friend from college. They'd met freshman year and roomed together for the next four years. Like sisters, they shared everything. It was Marsha who had told her, "sisters need not come from the same womb."

They sat in the cozy, pine paneled living room in front of a fire in the huge stone fireplace sipping tea while Nora told Marsha about the situation on Nantucket.

"The big house on Main Street, a cottage out at lovely Sconset, *and* a purse of cold cash. Oh, poor you. Decisions, decisions, for Nora to make." She feigned excessive drooling.

"Okay, wise guy, I came here for some sage advice, not smart ass digs."

"Speaking of sage, I have some lovely new candles a friend is making for the shop that, when lit, smell like Thanksgiving turkey cooking."

Nora told Marsha about Max. "Because I am just such a bad judge of that kind of person, I'm sure I've misread his attentions. I mean, he is so popular, so much fun, so self-assured and confident. He has dozens of friends who all adore him. Why would he be any more interested in me than he is in all the friends surrounding him? I think he is attentive to everyone. How would a woman judge whether he really liked her specifically or not? It is too ambiguous and I have too many big decisions to make without teasing myself and being disappointed."

Marsha's irrepressible grin wrapped itself around her facetious remark, "Oh right, sounds like a terrible man. So lacking in fine points. Wake up, girlfriend. Friends are one thing, Nora; a special woman is another. You said it looked like he was being pursued by that woman who went off to France, but he wasn't buying. And yet, he made an effort with you. What *does* it take to convince you? I wonder when you are going to realize that you are pretty special yourself. Any man would be lucky to win you, you're smart, successful, dependable, conscientious and, although I am fully aware that you are not cognizant of it, very beautiful. Go back there, open up the house, get a new job or open your own gallery. You can now that you are rich as Croesus, you know. You know the business inside and out. Start over. Grab Max and love him like crazy."

Marsha poured more tea from a hand-made stoneware teapot enveloped in a blue and white checked cotton tea cozy.

"Try one of my almond biscotti. I am experimenting with recipes. Give it a rating, one to ten."

It was so warm and loving in Marsha's antique house overlooking a wide salt marsh on the bay side of Barnstable. Cummaquid, designated a village rather than a town, being the smallest community on the Cape, sat in one of the loveliest stretches along the shore route. Marsha's house overlooked the bay and; across the harbor, the tiny grouping of cottages that hugged the shore of Sandy Neck. An old lighthouse and its keeper's house sat at the very end of the long sandy arm stretching into the bay. Long a place of fishing shacks, and since the thirties, a small community of summer cottages, which were the delight of every painter hoping to capture the true essence of Cape Cod.

Except for Aunt Bessie, it had been Marsha who could keep Nora grounded. Marsha had often come along to Nantucket with Nora on school vacations.

Since her marriage and the birth of her children and the time and attention demanded by her shop, they hadn't seen as much of each other. The occasional weekend when Nora drove down to the Cape was the best they could manage. However, they talked on the phone at least once each week.

Nora missed her best friend. Always, Marsha's advice was as good as gold. This time however, she just seemed to be suggesting too daring a scheme. She had been having some pretty delicious dreams about Max, but that didn't mean that he was dreaming about her, she knew.

"Look, sweetie, life is short. If you do not follow your dreams, even when they might be booby traps, you will remain in stasis, unfulfilled, stuck like a rock. No one would ever fall in love if we all hesitated when things didn't promise perfection. Go for it. Live there for a year. See if there is a gallery that will hire you. So what if you take a cut in pay, you can make it on what Aunt Bessie left you. One year. If Max turns out to be a sham, and the house is a money pit, you can always come back to Boston. With your reputation, any gallery will give you a job."

She left Marsha's house feeling braver and stronger. A plan developed as she drove back into the city. She'd get the gallery straightened out and hire someone whom she could begin to train to take her place if she decided to leave. She wouldn't leave her boss hanging after how good he had been to her. Come spring, she would take a weeklong vacation on Nantucket. At that time, she would give Max Michelson another appraisal. She would also check out the cottage out at Sconset that she hadn't seen in years because it was always rented out in summer.

FIVE

"As you can see, we have a number of regular artists whose work we show and then we also have one-person and group shows from time to time. The gallery has been here since Tim Acorn's father, Tim is my boss, opened it in the thirties. Tim went off to Europe right after college thinking he did not want to carry on the family business. He soon came back and the rest is history. When his father died, twenty years ago, Tim took over and although he doesn't spend a lot of time here- hence I have a job- he does love the place and I rely on him."

Speaking to a group of art students from the museum school, Nora was speaking honestly but cleverly covering for her boss who dreaded being stuck doing gallery duty if she had to be away. Not a people person and painfully shy, Tim Acorn was hardly suited to his inherited business, and had been greatly relieved when Nora took over completely allowing him to travel the world.

Nora always presented Tim in a favorable light. He was, after all, her boss and the gallery her comfortable security. Nora liked security and relative safety. Hence, her sluggish love life. Preferring a quiet night at home, reading, to the blind dates her friends offered or the dinner invitations from gallery clients whom she knew were married and on the prowl, her love life was nil. She would have liked a romance, a real romance, a storybook romance, with all the bells and whistles. The kind of feeling Max had brought out in her briefly.

The last man she had trusted had cleaned out her meager savings when he promised her a great return from a start-up company moving in from the west coast. He was newly working as a stockbroker when she trusted him because she was sleeping with him and believed in him. When the money disappeared, so did he. She'd survived and moved on. What else could she do? The man took off with her money and bruised her heart...not to mention her confidence in her ability to pick worthy men.

Back in Boston, Nora was back in her element. Here she was in full control; knowledgeable, reliable, respected by artists and clients alike. Back here in Boston, Nantucket, Viburnum Gate, and Max Michelson seemed like smoky images in a distant mirror.

Four months passed and spring popped overnight. The Boston Public Gardens burst into bloom and the swan boats returned to delight visitors to the lovely historic city by the bay. Nora was no closer to a decision about Nantucket as she walked through the Commons delighted by the sight of the tiny green shoots of daffodils and hyacinth piercing the warming earth. She loved spring. This spring however loomed like a kind of Sword of Damocles over her head. Memories of Christmas on the island loomed in a kind of misty unreality, no more real than if she had read about them in a book.

The charming but solidly geometric, patrician architecture the island, the beauty of its white sandy, windswept beaches, the stretches of grassy marsh and tranquil ponds called to her. Her last visit seemed more surreal than usual in her memory. Max seemed a dream, an unattainable dream, at best.

Nora loved Boston. The beauty of Back Bay, Beacon Hill, the lovely harbor islands, and nearby Cambridge with its charismatic Harvard Square, provided endless enjoyment. The little island of Nantucket still managed to hold tight to her heartstrings and beckon her back to its shores.

As a child, she had decided that she was an *island person*. Living on an island, as Aunt Bessie often said, was not for everyone, but island people knew who they were, and it "behooves them to find their island and settle in or be forever lost and at sea." Nora loved that sentiment.

Nantucketers called their island *the* island, as if there were no others. This, tantamount to a nationalistic attitude, was reinforced by their designation of everything across the water as "America." In fact, at one time during the Civil War, Nantucket attempted to secede from the union. When Nora was busy at the gallery, she was fully focused and thoughts of Nantucket receded to the back of her mind, sitting patiently on a shelf waiting to be taken down at a later time.

The air wafting in the open gallery door was soft and warm. The pot of paperwhites she had bought on her way to work that morning scented the area with a heady sweetness that some thought cloying. To her, the sweet scent was symbolic of spring. While the well-dressed man moved around the gallery looking at the latest group show, she watched him and sized him up. Nice looking in a sedate, businesslike way. Expensive dark gray suit, crisp maroon and white pin stripe shirt with a tie of the same colors but with wide maroon stripes. He exuded Brooks Brothers and GQ magazine. His short, well-cut salt and pepper hair suggested that he was probably in his mid-forties to early fifties. He smelled wonderful as he stopped to speak to her as he entered.

    She stood, as she always did after the initial introduction and explanation of how the gallery worked. Once she covered who they represented and told them about any special shows that were mounted that day, she slipped off, remaining silent and unobtrusive. It was her custom to allow clients to browse, knowing that she was available if they had questions.

    She liked herself in this setting. She was confident and self-assured. She wished she could always be this person. She was safe as the professional, competent gallery curator and manager. Unfortunately, whenever she tried to get into dating, she felt herself becoming someone she would find boring. Sure, she was bright and well educated, four years at Sarah Lawrence had added polish, and her knowledge of contemporary art was largely unsurpassed. Why then, should a man not find her interesting? She assumed that most men wanted a woman who was lots of fun, told funny stories, could take or leave a sexual relationship and move on when a better temptation appeared. Wasn't that how contemporary females were programmed? If so, then she was far too old fashioned to survive in today's dating world.

She knew she could not give herself to a man only to move on when the next sex partner came along. She wanted something deeper. Old fashioned was boring therefore, her poor record in the arena of dating.

"Pardon me. I guess I was wool gathering. I'm sorry, what did you ask me?" Nora had been caught daydreaming rather than doing her job of being alert without being obvious or hovering.

"I was just wondering what painting you like in this show. Although I suppose that is not fair of me to ask. You must have to remain impartial. Sorry, I take back my question."

The man stood with his arm crossed, studying the room. "I do like that one over by the column. The sky is fantastic isn't it? I've seen skies like that out west, in mountain country. Sometimes they are so bizarre, so gorgeous, you think that if someone captured them on canvas no one would believe them possible."

"Yes, I know what you mean. Do you think it might be sunset rather than sunrise? The title does not provide any hint, however. Marla Hutchins is a terrific painter. She is known for her skies. She lives in Colorado but comes east for the summer, staying at Cape Ann where she paints the sea and sky there. We have shown her seascapes, however this time we chose to stick with her work from out west. It is nice that you can relate, having traveled there."

"Actually, I grew up in New Mexico. Now there is a place for skies and a palette that will knock you out. I miss it."

Just then, two couples came in and Nora excused herself to greet them. She made it a firm point, of her way of doing business, to greet and chat with everyone, even if they looked as if they could never afford the gallery's exorbitant prices.

The man in the pinstriped suit was still there, still admiring the Hutchins paintings when she was ready to close up. He noticed the time, glancing at his watch and then at the grandfather's clock against the wall to be sure he was correct. "Sorry, I know you must be ready to head home. I've taken up enough of your time. I have enjoyed the work very much, and I would like to buy that one of Hutchins' with the wonderful sky. However, I don't want to pick it up until Thursday as I am staying at the Ritz and, although I am sure their security is fine, I'd rather not have it in my room."

"Would you prefer us to send it to your home or office? That might simplify everything. No problem, we do it all the time." Nora wondered if he might say something about it being a gift for his wife. He wasn't wearing a wedding ring but that certainly meant little these days. She knew that if she ever married she'd demand her husband wear one. There was one of those old-fashioned ideas again.

"That would be terrific. You can send it to my office in Philadelphia. I think I'll hang it there for a while. After all, I spend more time there than I do at home. That is, if you can call three rooms a home."

"Fine, just come into the office and I'll write out an invoice and get the mailing address." Nora decided that he was definitely not married and now she began to wonder what he did and why he was in Boston.

As if he'd read her mind, he said, "I get into Boston fairly often, we have a brokerage here and in Philadelphia so, I kind of move back and forth as needs be."

Their business completed, Nora walked him to the door and prepared to lock up. He turned as he stepped onto the sidewalk. "If you don't have plans for dinner, a husband, a boyfriend or a sick friend, would you join me at the hotel dining room? The food is damned good and I'll try to be entertaining. We could talk about skies, sunrise and sunset."

Nora decided to be spontaneous, why not? She had no plans and the Ritz dining room was hardly an offer to be turned down. She locked the gallery door and checked the alarm system. They walked the two blocks to the corner of Arlington and Newbury to the elegant Ritz Hotel. As they waited for their drinks, Nora's new acquaintance who had introduced himself as Adam Kendall, told her about his fear of flying and how he loved trains.

"I loved trains as a child when my mother and I would travel east from our home in New Mexico every summer to visit her family on the

Vineyard. I flew a lot for business in the beginning, but my claustrophobia just got the better of me, and I simply stopped. If I cannot get there by train, boat or taxi or, in a real pinch, a bus, then I simply don't go."

Seated by the window overlooking Arlington Street and the Boston Common they chatted about a variety of subjects. Adam made Nora feel that she was an interesting person. It certainly helped that he understood and loved art. After a delicious meal, coffee and after dinner drinks, they walked across the Commons. The night was soft as velvet, a perfect spring evening. Trees had started to green in the previous week. Everyone seemed to be afflicted with spring fever. It had been a long, cold winter. At the Frog Pond, Nora told Adam how she used to skate there as a child when she lived with her adoptive parents on Beacon Hill.

"One day, when I was a junior in college, they announced that they were both retiring and moving to the South of France. They are there now. I visited twice, but since then, with finishing college and getting started in my career, I haven't taken the time for many long vacations. I will go again though. I miss them. They were wonderful when my parents died. They were too busy to be full-time, hands-on parents but I knew they loved me and I had the housekeeper who mothered as much as anyone could need."

Adam told her he had to go back to Philadelphia and would be busy for a couple of weeks on some business that would take all of his time and energy but he'd call when he was returning to Boston.

The next morning, Nora received a letter postmarked Nantucket. The return address, professionally printed on the envelope, Martin House Inn, Center Street, Nantucket, MA took her by complete surprise.

Dear Nora, Quelle surprise! It is only I, Max from Nantucket . A couple of things: First, our dear friend, well, not exactly yours although as I told you, Michael developed a crush on you at Christmas, has passed away. It was tough sledding at the end and we all gathered around and ushered him into, we hope, a better place. Gad, how nice it must be to have such faith in the afterlife. Thought you would like to know.

Also, going through the attic at the inn I came across a painting that may interest you. It is by a fellow who was here painting in the twenties and I do not think he came to much fame. It is pleasant to look and well executed, although I am not an expert like you. On the back is penned, Viburnum Gate, Nantucket, 1927. It is obvious that it is your aunt's, sorry, your house on Main Street. The old moon gate covered in climbing viburnum could be none other.

Thought you might like it. I told the owners of the inn about it and they are not interested. They said I should give it to the new owner of Viburnum Gate. You. I can keep it here, ship it, or drop it off next time I am in Boston. Not that I have been there in the past hundred or so years but, life if full of surprises. Yours, Max Michelson

Nora sat down at the kitchen table and just looked at the letter as if it might reveal more of itself; perhaps tell her that Max had been thinking about her. Well, of course he had, the painting sparked his memory. Her house in the painting. Just a friendly, neighborly thing to do. She would have to write to tell him to keep it there and she would come by for it later in the spring or early summer when she planned to come over for a few days.

Bill Macy had called her recently to ask if she would like to rent out the 'Sconset cottage as Aunt Bessie had every summer. He told her that the income was sizeable and he would just deposit it in her Pacific National Bank account. He always screened the potential renters for her aunt, and Congdon Real Estate, who had the listing, could be relied upon to handle everything else.

She suddenly decided that she wanted to go out to check on the 'Sconset house before it was rented. She might want to remove some things or refurbish with new curtains or bedspreads. This call to action made her finally feel like a homeowner. Possession and pride. Most of all, she just wanted to get back to the island.

When her boss, Tim, decided to have the entire gallery repainted and the floors sanded and varnished, which would mean being closed for two weeks in early June, Nora made a plan. She would open up and air out the Main Street house that was probably pretty musty after being closed all winter. She could pick up the Viburnum Gate painting and see Max.

She hadn't heard from Adam from Philadelphia, so she'd crossed him off as a possible new lover. She wrote two short notes. One to Bill Macy telling him that she would be in residence at the Main Street house for two weeks in June and that she would like to rent the 'Sconset house for the summer season but she might be making some changes there before the tenants arrived. The other note was to Max thanking him for thinking of her regarding the painting of Viburnum Gate. She told him when she would be there, closing by adding that she looked forward to seeing him and his friends again.

SIX

The weeks leading up to Nora's escape from the city were hectic so the time flew. All the paintings in the regular collection had to be removed from the walls, dusted, frames checked and those that needed repair were sent to the man who did that work for them out in Winchester. Then, each was wrapped in special lint-free covering and taken up to the third floor storage room. The old gas operated elevator that had been installed when the building went up in 1919 had been removed because of safety issues, so Nora climbed the stairs many times…in her mind, at least a thousand times. She chalked it up to a great leg tightening and strengthening exercise.

Finally, the gallery was left in the hands of the painters. Tim left for the South of France and she headed for the ferry in Woods Hole. In the past, she'd always driven the extra miles to catch it in Hyannis just because it was traditional to do this. This time, she was anxious to get there and took the more expedient route.

The summer crowds had not yet formed so the ferry was reasonably quiet. She tried to concentrate on her book but she found her mind wandering. Once she had crossed Adam off the list of possible relationships, she had reassessed her life. She could thank him for that, she supposed. She felt better equipped to make the decisions awaiting her in Nantucket. Not that they would be any less painful, but they had to be made and she would no longer avoid them, they weren't going to go away just by ignoring them.

Stepping in the door of the old, musty, too-long closed up house, she set her duffel and laptop case down on the deacon's bench in the front hall and went directly to open all the windows. It was stifling and smelled of mothballs and dust.

Going from room to room, first floor and then second, not bothering with the attic, she could see that the caretaker had been there and put up the window screens. Evidence of mice was everywhere. She'd have to check to see what to do about the problem. She was an animal advocate, but somehow an infestation of mice flew below her radar of merciful live and let live.

The phone was working and she tested the lights. She'd have to take off the bed linens and the slipcovers her aunt loved to change with each new season. She knew that the upstairs cupboard held four seasons of them and they would all have to be aired before she chose a set for summer. Rugs that could be shaken would be, but the large Orientals would need professional cleaning. She was sure that Bill could recommend someone who did reliable cleaning on the island. Walking through the house, despite all the work she faced, she felt good. Really happy and anxious to take charge.

She took a small notebook from her purse and listed the things that would need doing if she was going to stay in the house. No worry about heat since spring seemed to be doing what it did about every decade in New England, swing right into summer with no setbacks.

The garden was overgrown and she'd noticed that the wild roses on the front had made insidious inroads into the frame of the screen door and found a little crack beside the inner doorframe that allowed entrance into the front hall. Aunt Bessie loved every age crack, slanted floorboard and quirky detail of the ancient house. She kept it up as much as she could with help from local tradesmen, but it was a never-ending battle.

She called Bill Macy's office phone and he picked up after the second ring. "Well, hello Nora, how nice to hear your voice. Well, well, two weeks on the old island, how very grand for you. What are your plans? If I may ask?"

"You certainly may ask Bill, first one is to take you to lunch at the Atlantic Café. Are you free?"

"I can be at twelve-thirty. That good for you?"

They set a date and Nora returned to her list. It suddenly occurred to her that the water might not be on so she headed for the kitchen to turn on the faucet. Nothing, not a drip. Shuffling through her notes, she found the phone number for Joshua Latham, the caretaker. He promised to be over within the hour to turn on the water. Nora asked him who to call about some minor repairs and he provided the name of a reliable handyman.

She recalled how her aunt always had red clay pots full of bright red geraniums filling the deep windowsills on the front of the house. Everyone passing by admired them. They seemed to bloom all year for Aunt Bessie who had two green thumbs.

Perhaps Bartlett's Farm had some red geraniums ready, and maybe she'd look for some black-eyed susans and sunflowers, as well, for the front garden. She remembered the huge faces of the sunflowers her aunt always grew. She'd never been a gardener, always living in the city as an adult, but she suddenly felt the urge to get out and work on her aunt's well-loved but now sadly neglected gardens.

But first, lunch. The Atlantic Café was busy, almost like summer, but she saw a lot of local faces as well. Even after the tourists invaded, the Atlantic was the favorite haunt of locals. She spotted Bill sitting at a table by the front window with a cup of coffee in front of him.

"Got away earlier than expected. Come, sit, the sun is warm here."

Bill rose to pull out her chair and she gave him a hug. He had morphed from complete stranger representing her aunt's will, to friend, helping her deal with all the hurdles after her aunt died.

"Well, you look just lovely Nora. How's the house? Been closed up a long time. I'm sure it is pleased to have you there. There I go anthropomorphizing inanimate objects.; old family habit or should I say, quirk?

"No problem, Auntie and I always did that. She'd talk to the old grandfather's clock convincing it to keep on ticking after what, two hundred and fifty years of faithful service? It would stop dead and not ring out its hourly carillon, and she would speak tenderly to it, and before you knew it, everything was just fine, again. We talked to squirrels and rabbits and even, once, a particularly colorful beetle in the kitchen sink. We are…were, just as quirky, so I understand."

Nora sat with her back toward the horseshoe shaped bar over which hung a collection of old objects, whaling harpoons, anchors, boat life rings, and assorted sizes of wooden blocks from ships. Turning to read the menu for the day's specials on a blackboard stand, she spotted him.

At the end of the bar, under the old mahogany canoe that hung from the ceiling as if having just crested a wave, he sat, laughing, entertaining and being entertained.

Max was listening intently to an attractive woman wearing a red Nantucket Marina baseball cap, a black Fog Island t-shirt and very short cut-off jeans shorts. Sensible Nora thought it was a bit early for shorts but…when in Rome. She knew that the unspoken Nantucket tradition was for flipflops to go on May first and not come off until November first, despite the occasional slog through chilling early snow.

Whatever the woman was saying, she had Max's full attention, there was no doubt about that. Now and then, he'd throw his head back and slap his thighs. He too looked like someone living on a tropical island that never saw winter. Clad in cut-offs and ripped t-shirt, his ragged flipflops looked to be held together with duct tape. His legs were tanned causing her to wonder if he'd slipped off to some sunny island for a month or so in the slow season.

Realizing that she'd been watching Max far too long, ignoring her lunch mate, she turned back to Bill, but not quickly enough.

Max turned, as if his head had been pulled by a string, attached to her optical nerves. Casually, he smiled and waved. Bill waved back, but Nora, feeling embarrassed, simply smiled. *Why do I let him turn me into a stupid teenager with a secret crush?*

Then, he simply turned back to the woman and continued talking. Nora's heart did a lurch and, in the full knowledge that she was jealous, she determined not to fall for a man who could have anyone he wanted. Damn him, she thought, *I will not let him get to me. I just have to remember what is important.*

Telling herself that her future did not hinge on a handsome, friendly, charming innkeeper who spends his time entertaining his massive audience in bars and restaurants. She considered that he'd probably never had a truly deep, meaningful relationship. *He probably prefers one night stands with no involvement anyway, so why do I waste my time thinking about him?*

"A penny."

"Oh sorry Bill, what were you saying?"

"You seem to be mesmerized. I don't suppose it is the décor or the delicious aromas emanating from the kitchen therefore…"

Embarrassed, caught in one of her woolgathering moments, she quickly turned back and looked down at the menu.

Max did not come over to their table and as the place filled up with the lunchtime crowd, her view of the bar became obstructed. She did not know when he left or if the woman went with him.

She walked back to the house determined to put Max Michelson from her mind. She did not need to be just one more of his women. She would like to get to know his friends better, but he would be hands off for her. His fun friends, minus dear sweet Michael.

Although the house was being warmed by the sun, she could still smell winter in the rooms. The unmistakable air of an uninhabited place that had not seen people for too long, she would have to dispel with lots of Murphy's Oil Soap. Time to head down to the A&P for sponges, mops and everything she would need to reclaim the house. She added to her list, pasta, rice, fresh veggies and fruit, salad fixings, olive oil and red wine vinegar, bread, butter, coffee and cream, a chicken for roasting and, with a stop at the fish market for scallops or maybe some filet of sole, she'd be ready for a stay.

Passing by the quilt folded on the back of one of the couches, the one close to the east window, she could see the still remaining gray cat hair from old Moses. Moses had died the week before her aunt. Bessie had called Nora in Boston to tell her the sad news and she had disturbed Nora by hinting that it might be time for her to go, as well. Moses had been there since Nora's fifth birthday when she and Bessie had gone to a shelter to pick out a companion for Bessie. "When you are not here, Nora, dear, this little furry fellow will keep me company."

She made one more check of the upstairs to determine what she'd need to clean up there. Stepping into her bedroom up under the eaves, two yellow button eyes stared at her from the blue and white quilted pillow sham. Her old teddy bear, Rugger, sat there, perched on the pillow waiting for her to return. Ratty, with patches of hair missing and stuffing peeking out from his left hand and right foot, he had waited for her, as he always did. Despite his condition, he looked, as he always had, contended with his life.

The curtains looked bedraggled because they hadn't had their annual spring wash and air-drying on the line in the backyard. The quilts also looked in need of a good airing on a breezy day. Moving into her bathroom, she saw that a talented spider had woven a lovely, intricate web in the corner of the old claw footed tub. In the lacy web were little tightly woven packages of unwary flies who had ventured into her territory.

She checked the closets and found her one blue ked that she had rescued when her catboat went over in a race and the other shoe had taken off, "Headed for Portugal," said Aunt Bessie, and they both laughed and went out to buy her another pair. However, she kept the lone shoe because she had worn them when she won a tennis match that summer. Summer dresses that no longer fit her, but from which she could not be parted, hung on hooks in the back of her closet. She spotted one turquoise bead that had fallen off of a pair of earrings that she had purposely, viciously, broken after Tim Coffin broke her heart. He had given her the earrings when they first fell in love. She was fourteen and he fifteen.

She hadn't been in the attic for years, so she thought about climbing the ladder, but then changed her mind. Another day.

Returning from the A&P with cleaning supplies, new mops and enough groceries for simple but fresh meals for at least four days, she set about unpacking. She made up her bed with fresh linens from the linen chest where they were always kept sweet smelling by lavender sachets. When they had last been laundered she did not know, but the lavender had, at least, prevented mold from taking over. They smelled like summers, Aunt Bessie and Moses. She clearly remembered the day the huge Maine coon cat had torn apart a lavender sachet and scattered the sweet smelling flowers all over the upstairs hall. Then, he decided to roll in it. For days, Moses smelled like a lavender plant and he seemed very much pleased with himself.

When the bed was freshly made with her favorite yellow and white checked sheets and the colorful crazy quilt she loved, she fell onto the bed. Next thing she knew, she was awakening and the room was darkening. The sun was just touching down on the horizon and sending out flames that cut through deep purple shadows. Although the house was quiet, she could hear the wood of the house relaxing after a warm day. A muffled crack, first here and then there, as beams and joists settled in for the night. From beyond the edge of the bedside table but not as far as the windowsill, she could hear the low-key buzz of a fly that, she imagined, having escaped the treacherous trap laid by Mrs. Spider, was attempting to lay low. Aunt Bessie had taught her to listen, *"Really, really listen. Far below the cacophony of daily life there is a delicate rhythm of secondary life to be heard."*

Also, she had taught her to make up stories about animals, her pets and the chipmunks, squirrels and rabbits in gardens of Viburnum Gate. Together, they had given them personalities and personal stories. Nora imagined the cagey fly lying low hoping to escape the clutches of the busy spider. Waiting, listening and hoping for a better fate than its companions. Likewise, she wondered if the house was holding its breath, waiting for her to decide its fate.

SEVEN

"Good morning, The Martin House Inn, Max speaking."

"Good morning Max, it's Nora Kavanagh over at Viburnum Gate." Thanks to the protection of the phone, Nora felt as if she sounded self-assured and businesslike.

"Well, welcome back. Are you staying at your house for the summer?"

"Oh no, just for two weeks while my gallery, the gallery where I work in Boston, is having some renovations done and then I head back to the city. I am calling to see if you might have the time to show me the painting of my house that you found in your attic. I thought I would do some research into the artist. Bill Macy said that he has heard of him and that he was here in the twenties but he doesn't think he achieved much recognition. I have yet to check with the Artists Association."

"Well," Nora could hear the smile in his voice, "I think I am growing fond of the picture. I have it on a stand just beyond the kitchen half wall and I look at it often. The artist certainly captured the gate, the fence, and the architecture of the old house."

Nora could not imagine what to say. Did he mean that he had changed his mind and wanted to keep it? Instead, he added, "Good thing that you are here. I should be gone soon."

"You are leaving the island, Max?"

"No, but the inn is for sale and if I can't put together a solid group of financial backers to buy the place, I will be looking a new job. But that's another story entirely. Why don't you come over for tea tomorrow? Iced I would suggest, considering the weather. Never remember summer coming so early or so earnestly. This kind of weather usually arrives around the middle of July."

Well, she had her answer. The painting was to be hers.

"Sure, that would be fine. I remember a hot June when I was twelve. My aunt would soak a bed sheet in the icy water from the hand pump in the shed, wring it out, and throw it over my pajama-clad body in bed. At first I'd flinch, then it started to feel soooo good. What time would you like me to be there?"

"Let's say eleven, if you are free. My morning will have cleared up by then, guests fed, dishes in the washer, my tenth cup of coffee settled in my stomach, producing prodigious acid."

"Sounds like you'll need warm milk rather than tea," Nora smiled as she said this remembering a communications course she had in college in which she learned that smiles can be "heard." Radio broadcasters learn the technique so that the audience can pick up their verbal mood clue.

"Got a cast iron stomach, fortunately. Iced tea it will be. At eleven. I suppose you like scones hot from the oven. See you then, Nora." He hung up and Aunt Bessie's voice floated through her mind. *"Never let a man absorb you. Do not take on his life, his ideas and his attitudes. Never give away your own identity. Keep this firm in your mind; you should run from any man who expects you to.*

Grabbing her cell phone, Nora punched in Marsha's number. Time for a pep talk. An hour later, she felt great. Marsha reminded her of her talents, capabilities, strong character, good values and "Knock out looks".

The next day, at precisely eleven, dressed in crisp white shorts, a tangerine colored cotton t-shirt and white sneakers, Nora headed up Center Street toward the Martin House Inn. Two new friends about to view an interesting piece of art. No risk in that. She had tried her hair down and then pulled it into a ponytail for a more casual look. Now, she was ready to face Max Michelson, friend to friend. Nothing more.

Waiting on the front porch, his hair also in a ponytail, wearing khaki shorts and a much washed, soft to the point of ready to become a dust rag, white Izod shirt, sat Max. A large pitcher of iced tea, covered in condensation, sat on a wicker table with a matching chair to each side.

"Hi, neighbor." Max rose to greet her, gently kissing her cheeks European style. At least it was a real kiss and not an air kiss.

The temptation to turn abruptly and cause a collision of their mouths was strong. Luckily her pragmatic self won the battle with her romantic self.

Handing her deftly into a wicker chair, he said, "Do you know that here on the island, even if you live way out at 'Sconset, you are still considered a *neighbor* to us town mice?"

"That's what I love about the island, the sense of really belonging."

"Well, what are you doing, this visit? Redecorating, and reclaiming your house?

"I'm doing lots of cleaning and re-organizing, hoping the process will aid me in making certain decisions I ought to be making about the future of the property. More appropriate work for a winter day than this tropical heat wave we are having, I must admit. "

"Yup, this summer is obviously going to be a real scorcher. A sand burner, as the islanders say. By the way, allow me to apologize for not coming over to the table the other day at the Atlantic when you and Bill came in. I was deep in a financial discussion with a potential backer for the purchase of the inn. Lots to catch you up on since you were here at Christmas. By the time we finished our discussion, the place was so packed and the woman had to get to the ferry, so I just left to drive her down."

"Oh, not at all. Bill and I had business to discuss as well. You waved. That was nice."

"Didn't want you to think me impolite, my sainted mother would eschew such poor manners."

Nora wished she had something fascinating to say, but she had nothing. They weren't close enough to get into a discussion of how difficult it was deciding what to do with the old house she so loved. Her work stories would not interest Max, and they had no mutual friends. Max deftly handled the silence that had fallen between them.

"Hey, come on inside, I have the painting lying on the desk in my office. You should love it. The time period appears to be sometime in the thirties, going by the style alone. Kind of misty and overly sentimental. Again, I'm no authority on painting, that's your job, but I do think the guy had some talent."

They went inside. The place was quiet, obviously all the guests were gone for the day or, it being only June, there were no guests.

Max's office was neat and tidy, Nora noted. Max stood back as she leaned down to inspect the small painting framed in a wide, intricate art nouveau style gold frame. "It is in excellent condition, considering its age. Hasn't faded at all, I'd say. Either it was hung on a wall that got no direct light or, was hidden away. Well," she turned to Max, "I don't mean surreptitiously necessarily, stored away when perhaps the style was no longer au courant. Art lovers are finicky. Art does go out of style, ending up in attics awaiting a resurgence of its style. When a style comes back into vogue, suddenly the old stuff gains new value."

As she always did when looking at a new painting, she tried to imagine the artist. "What, if anything, *do* you know about the artist, Max?"

"Not a hell of a lot. I asked around, and the only person who could tell me anything was Adele Macy. Distant aunt or cousin to Bill, I believe. Well, all the Macys are related, of course. She's our octogenarian island history buff. A terrific old lady with lots of spunk. She hinted that she knew the guy quite well. Got a kind of twinkle in her eye when she told me that he was living on the island in the late twenties and early thirties. She has some stories that need to be delved, I'd say. All she would add was that eventually he headed to New York."

"Did he ever return, did she say?"

"Nope. She was pretty cagey about the man. I'll bet my boots that she, as my grandmother used to say, 'stepped out' with him and maybe more. I thought she had nothing more to say about him, then, just as I was getting ready to leave, she said something else. 'I knew him in New York, later, just before the war. He was a good friend of the painter Edward Hopper and his wife, Jo. By then, he'd become quite eccentric…although he was still dashing.'

"She sounds fascinating. It would be fun to see what else she might reveal if inspired to talk about him. By the way, what is the artist's name? I cannot read this scrawled signature."

"Simon Graystone. Kind of a cryptic kind of name, don't you think?"

"Hm. Interesting name. Don't think I've ever run into it. Maybe he stopped painting when left here and got an *honest* job."

"Could be. Got to keep the wolf from the door, you know." Max laughed and stepped closer. "You ought to talk to Adele. She'd appreciate your background, she's a serious art lover. She might open up to you, Nora…Worth a try, anyway."

"Do you suppose my aunt knew her?"

"Damn, just remembered what else she told me. Her parents used to own the Wauwinet Inn and she still lives in the family home out there. She told me that your Aunt Bessie waitressed at the inn when Adele did in her teens. Her parents insisted that she work although they were quite well to do. She liked your aunt a lot. I think they were in school together, as well.

Max stood close beside Nora, leaning over to better look at the painting. "The gate looks like it was just recently installed about that time. Freshly painted, at least. The viburnum bushes are young saplings aren't they? No one ever sees that side of the house from the street because of the way the bushes have taken over. It is a lovely moongate isn't it? Would be nice to prune it back a bit."

"That's just what I was thinking, such a waste to leave it so hidden. It seems that it might have been put there solely for the occupants of my house to walk into their neighbor's yard. There never was a lane there as far as I know. Look here," pointing to a sliver of the corner of the house next door caught in the picture, "the neighbor's garden comes right up to the hedges."

Nora felt Max's warm closeness. The room was hot and little air filtered in through the two-screened windows beyond which she could see high, overgrown lilac bushes. His close proximity brought back an elusive memory of her father's Old Spice aftershave. Catching her breath, she locked her knees to keep them from turning to jelly. Then, she saw something that took her completely by surprise.

"Look, there is someone in the doorway leading to the side porch. Tough to see, but I am sure it is a woman. See." Nora pointed to a hazy image.

"Yeah, the artist seems to have wanted to include her but not let her draw attention away from the moongate." Max leaned down so that his nose nearly touched the painting.

"Have you got a magnifying glass, Max?" Nora stood up straight, stretched her neck that was feeling the effects of being bent over the painting. Also, she needed to move away from Max; the pull of his body, his smell, the fact that she wanted to reach over and touch him was becoming too much to resist.

"Sure, somewhere. Look in that middle drawer, I'll check out at the registration desk. I think I used it recently to read a name that was tough to discern. Oh, here it is. Take a look."

Nora leaned back over the painting and the glass helped her to see much more clearly the woman in the doorway. "Well, of course, it must be. It looks like Aunt Bessie although, of course, I never saw her so young and lovely. I guess the painter, this Simon

Graystone, wanted to please Aunt Bessie by including her without making her the focus of the painting. That would be typical of her. Always in the background but the mover and shaker that everyone depended upon."

"How about that, an early picture of your aunt. Now, we nosy folks want to know what was the relationship between her and Simon Graystone? Adele, Bessie and Simon."

"Just keep your nasty thoughts to yourself, Mr. Michelson. People behaved better back then."

"No, they just didn't advertise their peccadillos, Ms. Kavanagh."

"Mind scrubbed clean."

"Wait a minute. Why was the painting here rather than at my, Aunt Bessie's, house? Wouldn't he have painted it on commission for someone in my family? Aunt Bessie's parents, I would expect. Do you have that information, Max?"

"As a matter of fact I do. It seems, according to Adele, this was a private home and the artist rented a room from the Martin family. Evidently, he never delivered the painting. Maybe he was not happy with the result. We will never know. Sorry, I don't have more for you, Nora."

"Oh, not at all. This will be fun. Art detective work is what I thrive on."

He looked at her in a way she could not translate, a mix of admiration and jest. Was he laughing at her although he realized that she was good at her work? Would she ever just know what he was thinking or always go on wondering? Perhaps that was part of his fatal charm. He probably worked at being an elusive enigma.

"When should I try to see Adele?"

"Not for a few days, she's visiting a sick friend over in America. In the meantime, we can go to see my good pal Mabel Austin who is the keeper of the records at the library. Anything and anyone who has ever touched foot on island soil shows up in her records. In another time, she'd be the lone telephone operator through whom all calls had to pass and all gossip was disseminated. Mabel is not a gossip, but she does know everything about everybody. I want to be as spry and wiry at eighty-four. You will love Mabel."

"Sounds like a good first step."

"How about tomorrow morning, an expedition into the bowels of the old Atheneum library building? If nothing else, it will be cool down there in the stone basement."

They laughed and set a date for eleven thirty the next day, allowing time for Max to get his guests on their way after breakfast. She recalled that he had mentioned having some guests. It was early in the season, however the Nantucket tourist season had been, in recent years, stretching on both ends like an expanding universe.

She hoped that she and Max were not stuck in alternate universes incapable of ever meeting or overlapping. Maybe it was a healthy start to be sharing a fascinating art research project.

EIGHT

"Hello, Maxwell, how's the inn business? I heard the inns and B&B's are booking lots of reservations for the summer season. Good to hear. It's always a long winter for local businesses. Of course, it is our busiest season. Long winter nights for reading. What can I do for you today, Max? Got some great new mysteries just in."

"Yes, Katrin, it looks like a promising season. Still working on a Dan Brown, his first one, lesser known, but really good. I'll be in when I finish it. Is Mabel here? We made a loose appointment for this morning."

Max introduced Nora to Katrin. "Our trustee Bessie's niece. So nice to meet you, Nora. We certainly miss Bessie. She was in here all the time. Checking up on us, making sure we were taking good care of *her* library. Do you have a library card?"

"Yes. I've had one since I was a kid. I spent every summer here and school vacations. This place feels like home. Best library anywhere."

"Well Max, if you don't require reading material, then I guess I have to send you along to Mabel."

Another one of Max's admirers, Nora noted.

"Oops, I steered you wrong. The schedule says that Mabel is on her break. She walks over to the Hub for the paper and then takes a spin around the block. She's been having some trouble with her hip, so she doesn't walk as far as she used to. The doctor says it's good to exercise it a little but not overdo. Doc wants her to have a replacement. She's stubborn, as you know, she's sure it's just a matter of time and the hip will settle down and behave again. Refuses to believe the doctor."

"That's our Mabel."

"Why don't you two browse, she ought to be walking in any minute."

Max thanked Katrin and pointed Nora in the direction of the reading room. "Want to show you some excellent sketches done by a cabin boy on one of the whaling vessels. I think you will appreciate them."

As they walked away from the circulation desk, the librarian called after them, "By the way Max thanks for the lovely nut bread. Mother loved it, once she was able to take nourishment again. Ever thought of opening a bakery?"

Max turned and gave her one of his wonderful smiles. "Could happen, one of these days, Katrin." Nora watched this exchange feeling a little envious of the closeness of the island's people, Max's far-reaching popularity and all the friends who got to enjoy that smile every day. Her eyes stuck to Max's mouth knowing she wanted more than a simple smile; she wanted to kiss Max and never stop kissing him.

"Nora, wake up. Come on, let's look at those sketches."

"Hmm? Oh, sorry, didn't mean to stare. Just thinking about things I want to do to my house." She stumbled through her explanation for staring at him hoping he'd just think she'd gone off on a daydream while he spoke to the librarian.

"Mabel used to ski competitively when she was young. She sky-dived for her seventieth birthday. I think she has been married six or seven times, three times to the same man. But perhaps I shouldn't tell you all of this. I'm sure, she will tell you herself, eventually. That is if you stick around long enough."

"I can't wait to meet this paragon."

They sat over the fine sketches safely kept under glass along with the story of the young boy who went to sea at fourteen and did not return home again for eight years. His sketches told the real story of life aboard ship, not the romantic adventure so many young boys expected to live.

Heading back to the foyer, Nora saw a petite, white-haired woman dressed in a flowered dress, a pearl choker and sensible shoes with a kneepad in place on her left leg.

"Max my dear, how lovely, not too busy to see your old friend and best girl, how very nice. And, you have brought a friend." Leaning down to hug Mabel, Max gently lifted her off her feet a few inches and she squealed with delight.

"Put me down you damned fool, silly boy. What will the ladies and patrons say?"

Nora watched their bantering and laughed at the scene.

She took Nora's hand in both of hers and the déjà vu instant almost brought Nora to tears. Soft and warm, Mabel's hands felt just like Aunt Bessie's. "I sometimes wonder why I keep the old house since I'm rarely there. This old place is more home to me than it is. You know, they just cannot function without me and so here I am every day and into the night."

Turning to Nora, Max laughed and added, "Not the way I hear it. These young people and even old Bentley the janitor would love to get her off their backs. She's an albatross."

Mabel laughed at his remark and poked him gently on the arm. "So, you are my dear friend Bessie's niece. We never met because during your childhood I was away. I went to Australia with my last husband. When he died, I returned home. Well, I suppose you require my services, dear girl, since obviously it was not my charms that drew this naughty boy."

Nora got a kick out of being called a girl. An octogenarian needn't be held to task for the outdated term, politically incorrect or not.

"Max discovered a painting done probably in the twenties or thirties of Viburnum Gate. I'd love to know more about the artist."

"Sounds like fun. Let's go to my office and begin the search." Turning to Max she said, "And I suppose you can come too, if you promise not to touch anything." Laughing together, Max and Mabel could have been lovers but for the age difference. Mabel led them down the stairs. Max suggested the elevator, but Mabel scoffed at such a foolish idea, "Elevators are for the aged."

Down in the archives in the basement, Mabel led them to a huge cupboard filled with labeled boxes explaining that these records contained the facts on every painter who had ever depicted the island on canvas. "We have worked diligently with the Artists Association recording this information. Of course, the twenties and thirties brought a number of artists to our shores. Suddenly, we were the hot place to paint. What is the name on your painter?"

"Simon Graystone."

"Sounds familiar."

"He painted Viburnum Gate so beautifully. Captured all the charm of the old moongate and the hedge in full bloom. My aunt may have been captured by his brush, standing in the doorway in shadow."

"That is it, I presume, covered up with one of the inn's dishtowels, Max?"

Max unwrapped the painting and placed it a table covered in green felt, evidently as protection for old records studied there.

She took a deep breath and sat down in a nearby chair. "Oh, my, how lovely. What a treasure for you, Nora."

"Do you think we might find some information on the artist, Mabel?"

"We can certainly try. Reach up there, Max, bring down that box marked nineteen twenty-five to nineteen forty. That would be the period for this type of work. Sentimental and dreamy, a nice period for art. Well," she turned to Nora as Max reached for a large cardboard box, "so, you will be coming to live at Bessie's house, child."

"Oh, no, I live and work in Boston. I am trying to decide what to do about the house here. I love it but I am not sure I can afford to live on the island."

"I know. Young people have to leave to find work. Darned shame. Who will keep up the old places if all the youngsters must leave? Only the old moneyed families will provide new keepers. Take my advice, dear, hang onto Viburnum Gate if you possibly can. Ah, thanks, Max. Open it up and let's begin."

Mabel's words swept over Nora like a winter chill. One-half of her head told her that she had to hang onto the house no matter what, even choosing to survive on Spam and cold cereal. The other, the more practical half, warned her that she could spend the rest of her life in penury if she even tried.

"Shall we put it on the table over here, Mabel? The lighting looks good over here. How's this?"

"Just lovely. Now let's see." Mabel lifted three plump manila folders out of the box, and chose the one marked Painters of the twenties. Carefully, as Max and Nora watched, Mabel went through the names that were, fortunately, in alphabetical order.

Coming to nineteen twenty-eight, she stopped and pulled out a few clipped together pages. "Aha, that's why his name sounded familiar. Oh, this brings it all back. Bessie and Adele and I all had crushes on this so bohemian man. He was tall and fair-haired, very slim, almost gaunt, probably didn't eat much. Lived on the sale of a few paintings. Probably only when he did a commission, did he make any real money. Naturally, back then, we did not have a gallery every ten feet along Main Street and all the side streets off Main. We were not the art mecca we are today, certainly. He went off to Boston, I recall, hoping for better luck. Yes. Hmm. He was charming. He liked Bessie best, I recall. Never could understand why she didn't just throw it all over and go off with him."

"Probably because she liked regular meals and living in a place without cockroaches rather than a cold water artist's garret," Max laughed and Mabel joined in.

Nora tried to see he aunt, who had been old as long as she could remember, as a young woman. Even old, she was lovely…soft, unlined skin and lots of snow white hair. In love with an artist, but afraid to give up her good life at Viburnum Gate.

"Do you think Aunt Bessie returned his love, Mabel?"

"Hard to know. Bessie was pretty circumspect. She and Adele and I were best friends but she was never fully open about her feelings. She kept a lot to herself. Kind of the family way with the Folgers. Which brings to mind a story about your family. It would have been when Bessie was a girl. Her father, Henry Folger Beechmont, took in a distant cousin who came to his door with a sad story. Her name was…ah, yes, Laura. She had taken up with a sailor by the name of… Oh, yes, Max, you and he share a name. Homer Maxwell it was. He was here for a time on a ship out of New Bedford. The ship limped in with a broken mast and was laid up at Gray Lady Shipyard.

"She was with child by the time he shipped out and she came to Henry's door with her sad story. She slipped away one night when the child was a toddler and no one ever heard from her again. I believe the child was also called Laura. Or maybe I've got that wrong. Oh, my, I hate what happens to the brain's retrieval system in old age."

Turning her attention back to the records, she ended her story.

"Maxwell, interesting. My name, Maxwell, my mother told me, was an old family name. To add irony, my mother was Laura. Just coincidence, my roots are definitely not planted in Nantucket soil."

Nora only half listened. Her mind was working on the elusive artist and his work.

"I'd love to see more of Simon Graystone's work, Mabel. Any idea of where it might be? Probably, some of the old families right here on the island have his paintings hanging on their walls."

"Probably more likely stored away in dank attics, unfortunately, Nora. This style has been out of fashion for some time. Someone might know however. Hmm, I wonder."

"I caught that pregnant pause, Mabel. You are keeping something from us. What is it?"

"Oh, just something I remembered. Not my place to share though. Might be worth a try nevertheless. Maybe she is old enough to want to get it off her chest. I wonder."

Nora looked at Max and he winked. "Okay, old woman, cough it up. You know something tasty and you are being pretty darned cagey. Who is she and what might she want to get off her chest?"

"Okay, but do not tell her I told you or she will never speak to me again."

"That's a start. We promise. Now how about her name so we can not tell her you told us."

"Before that, Mabel, just one thing I'd like to know. When was the moon gate added?"

"It was Henry III's gift to his little daughter. Bess was born on the night of a full moon and the next day he hired a local carpenter to add the fence and the moongate. Sweet, wasn't that? Your mother's family lived just down the street from Bess's family. You do know that Bess and your grandmother were cousins, so she really wasn't your aunt, don't you?"

"Yes, my mother always called her aunt and that was what she was to me, Aunt Bessie."

"Okay, old woman, a name please." "Adele Macy."

NINE

"Perhaps something scandalous?" Max made a dramatic flourish and Mabel looked enigmatic.

"I can only tell you that Bess ran into Simon in New York, years later. She said he was still pretty dashing. But that is for her to tell you, if she chooses to."

Leaving the Atheneum after, thanking both Mabel and Katrin, who once again received one of Max's great smiles, Max and Nora stepped out into the sunshine. The air had cooled slightly and seemed less humid. Any bit of relief was welcome. Summer was coming on early and strong.

"How about we get some sandwiches and cold drinks and let me show you a very special place?" Max beamed one of those delicious smiles at Nora and she dumbly nodded acquiescence.

"Don't you have to be back at the inn? You've been so generous with your time helping me and introducing me to adorable Mabel, but you must not let me keep you from your work."

"Melanctha is on duty, so, I am free until breakfast tomorrow." Max said this with a look that weakened Nora's knees and elicited a visceral response in her solar plexus. She wondered if he meant more than that he had a little extra time. *Do not read anything into his words.*

They bought huge aromatic sandwiches at the Even Keel and packed them and a half dozen assorted flavors of Nantucket Nectar drinks into the back of Max's truck in a cooler that was conveniently supplied with ice. Nora wondered when he had put the ice in the cooler and how much he was controlling how this day went. Did he really plan all this, while presenting it as spontaneous? She liked the idea and had no intention of being a spoilsport.

They headed out of town toward Tom Nevers Head. On the way he told her how the airport and the old air base had been named after old Tom Nevers, a native man who worked for the government during WWII, spotting planes and generally doing his patriotic duty from their small island. The beach at the "head" spread out forever. The swath of white sand and sparkling water with low white fringed waves rolling in, was the perfect place for a picnic. Other than the seagulls soaring overhead, occasionally dropping a closed clam or mussel hoping to crack it open, they were totally alone.

They spread out the L.L. Bean blue and black checkered fleece blanket Max said he always kept in the truck "for unexpected, spontaneous picnics or emergencies." Nora wondered if this was a little of both.

They walked the beach, collected seashells, ate their delicious lunch and then, as they lay on their backs watching the gulls dive and swoop, Max asked

Nora if she was involved with anyone. Nora's first reaction was to want to say, "No, free as a bird."

Deciding that sounded a little too needy, she simply told him that she had recently ended a relationship. No need to tell him that the next to last bastard had pretty much cleaned out her bank account by recommending investments that never panned out, and the last had just faded into obscurity.

"Never been married? A great looking, talented, successful woman like you and no dark past, no still salivating ex-husband hoping to win you back?"

"Nope, no dark past. A simple, straightforward life with no secrets. Just working long hours, forgetting to take vacations, going home every night to my cats and a good book. Have you been married Max?"

"Yes, once. For about twenty minutes. No, to tell the truth, it was really eight and a half months. I have a daughter, Jennie. She's fourteen. I split from her mother almost thirteen years ago. She was born in Puerto Rico where her mother went to run a big hotel. We met in hotel management school and married because she was pregnant. Honorable man that I was, I made an honest woman of her. Bad mistake on both our parts. That's it."

"Do you see your daughter?"

"Not as much as I'd like to. She's a great kid. A real beauty, smart and talented. She does great sketches she sends me of the island. One island to another, as we say. She needs to be more challenged and her school isn't doing that. I've suggested to

Miranda that she could come here for high school. Miranda is a great mother, really attached to Jennie and, afraid to let her go, I know. However, I want her to get the best education possible. Tried to compromise with a private school in the states. Not exactly budget wise, but I'd eat dog food if it meant she'd get a quality education. She will have to leave there for college, so, I'm working on Miranda to make the break now, for Jenny's sake."

"Do you visit her?"

"I spent about six weeks there right after I lost my job, before the Martin House hired me." *So that's where he was for his mental adjustment,* Nora noted.

The warm sun, the salt air, sandpipers dancing along the shore and two people so close with no one around for miles. Nora felt as if she'd been transported to a dessert island with this man whose body called to her. She considered what a more aggressive woman might do in such a circumstance. She however, was not an aggressive woman.

When Max rolled over onto his side to face Nora, and she knew the kiss was coming, she heard the bells and whistles women who read romance novels were told to expect.

The next sound was that of the happy children's voices filling the air as they bounded down the beach. Kiss interuptus. Max sat up and looked around. He waved to the man leading half a dozen children down the beach right toward them. Nora quickly sat up, straightened her t-shirt and short skirt and blushed from ear to ear.

"Hey Ned, looks like you've got an enthusiastic group. Are you cleaning the beach today or doing a nature study?"

"Hallo Max," the bearded man said in a crisp British accent; "today it is a bit of this and a bit of that. When we spot some trash washed up, we clean, when we spot turtle tracks, we make note of their whereabouts. Ridleys you know. On the endangered list, poor buggers. We need more study to determine their fate however. In addition, I and the scamps are learning about the shorebirds' nesting and mating habits..."

The man gave Nora a look that was full of humor, and maybe a touch of apology for breaking up their tete-a-tete.

"as well as danger from predators to eggs and such. The *whole enchilada* as they say. City children these are, so I've got to get them involved in saving the planet you know."

"And you do a great job, Ned. Hi kids. Listen to this man, he knows all about the beaches. Enjoy the day." Max reached a hand down to Nora and she grabbed it and stood, smiling at the children who had nearly gotten an explicit lesson in human mating habits right there on that L.L. Bean blanket.

Laughing, Nora and Max loaded the picnic paraphernalia into the truck. Max took her in his arms as they closed the back flap. With this kiss, the music and fireworks recommenced.

After the kiss, Max held her close, his face in her hair that had fallen out of the ponytail while they lay on the beach and which she hadn't bothered to restore. He had said, when it hit her shoulders, "Don't tie your hair up again. You look like a mermaid. Nora, the Nantucket mermaid."

"Max I..." but that was all she could get out beyond the lump in her throat. At last, kisses that measured up to those in books.

"Whatever you are about to say, that I can pretty much predict from what I have observed about the way your mind works, don't. Don't list the reasons why this will not work. Just remain in the moment, Nora."

Driving back to town, Max told her funny stories about inn keeping, the odd people you meet and the romances begun between singles who meet by chance. He listed the kinds of catastrophes he'd encountered like plugged up toilets and a leaking roof that spilled water onto the bed of newlyweds. He told her he ought to get back to give Melanctha some time off. "Even though we will be having no guests until the weekend, we have a lot of work to do to get ready for the summer rush."

The small talk continued all the way back into town as Nora shared her plans for the old house if she could swing the expense. If she decided to keep it. Max reaffirmed Mabel's advice that she should do anything she could to hold onto the old family home. She wished it were that easy as just wanting it very much.

Strange, thought Nora as she entered through the kitchen door of her house, how one minute you can be inches away from making love and the next minute the spell is broken and it's just small talk like it never happened.

As they'd parted, Nora told Max that she fully intended to research the painter, Simon Graystone, through the channels she used in her work. "Wouldn't it be great to have a retrospective on his work? Find it all and get it on loan."

"Yup. Unless he only painted three pictures. See you, Nora, great day. Got to do it again, real soon."

Standing in the sunlit kitchen, smelling the lavender she'd hung on the wall and put in potpourri holders, she felt contented. Perhaps, something might yet grow between her and Max. Perhaps she'd find a way to showcase the painter who had so lovingly depicted her house and her aunt. Perhaps, it occurred to her, Bessie might never have noticed herself standing in the deep shadows. It had taken Nora a close inspection with a magnifying glass to identify a woman there. She would begin by calling a man she knew in Boston who was an expert on obscure, twentieth century painters.

The following morning, as she was having coffee in the garden, Marsha called. "How's the new romance going? Oh, and of course, the house decisions?"

"Oh Marsha, I am so confused. First, the house decision is going nowhere. The more I walk around and remember the good times here, the less I want to let it go. But that's just kidding myself. Most certainly, I cannot afford to live here. What would I do for work? The romance is also a mystery yet to be unraveled. One, no two, lousy kisses...well, actually they were unbelievable, but probably meaningless. At least for him. For me they could have been a proposal of marriage. I am still sure that Max is a player. I'm not too sure what that that means but, you know, he's not available and not interested."

"Okay, so move on. Anyone else you've got your eye on out there in Americana Disneyland?"

"No. I just have to figure out what I am going to do or not do. Dear, sweet Bill Macy, my attorney, keeps reminding me that I do not really have to do anything for a while. But, you know me, inaction makes me very nervous.

"How old is this Macy guy?"

"Oh, Marsha, no, he's like a kindly uncle. Nothing there at all except that he is no nice and so considerate and so helpful. He's probably just few years older than me, but no. Just don't see him in that light."

"Hey listen to yourself. You just described the perfect husband material. Is he single? Maybe it is time to adjust your light, woman."

"Well, yes, but he...well, I just don't think about him in those terms."

"Well, honey chile, maybe you ought to check your thinking some and get on with finding yourself someone before all your eggs atrophy, your boobs hit your waist and your wrinkles have wrinkles of their own. Love ya. Got to go, Timothy just put a live frog in the bowl of pasta salad."

Nora laughed at Marsha's nonchalant attitude to things like a frog in the pasta salad. She could never be a mother, she assured herself, such things would have her tearing out her hair.

TEN

Back in Boston, after a great vacation on Nantucket, Nora threw herself into work at the gallery getting ready for a new exhibit. She had to decide between four artists whose agents all wanted the gallery to show their client's work. It was difficult however for her to pull her attention away the sheets faxed from Abram Gillespie in New York. A renowned expert on obscure, little known, either for the lack of work still extant, or lack of recognized talent, artists.

Simon Graystone however, appeared to have been very talented, although his work, according to Abram, "disappeared for the most part. One source was helpful in listing fifty-three of his paintings in a book put out by the New York Society of Early Twentieth Century American Artists. Where they went, I cannot imagine. He only showed in two New York galleries, from what I can tell. Got good reviews, but never really made the big time. One small mention of his having spent a few summers painting on Nantucket…no listing of what he did while there. Wish I had more for you, Nora."

Nora turned to the last page, an addendum Abram had added. Shortly after her aunt died, Nora was at a conference with Abram and she mentioned wanting to find the time to look deeper into her island roots. Evidently, the clever researcher had done some of that for her. He'd attached the following.

"In 1970, a woman named Annabelle Henderson from Portland, Maine, while doing some genealogical research into her family roots, put together enough information to prove that she was related to a woman named Laura Folger Maxwell from Nantucket." Nora recalled Mabel mentioning a Laura who had been left on her own, pregnant and destitute. She was forced her to seek out a distant relative for help for herself and her child. Aunt Bessie's father. At the time, she'd been more interested in what could be learned about Simon Graystone and the name slipped to the recesses of her mind.

Now, she remembered that Max said his mother was also Laura and Maxwell was an old family name. Interesting. Was it too much of a coincidence that she and Max might be blood relatives? At least, based on what Mabel said about the young woman being a distant cousin, they wouldn't be that close. A hint of panic had to be quickly squelched as a client stepped into her office wanting to buy a painting. She would think about that later.

On a hot July day, disregarding the fact that the accountant was breathing down her neck to get the books to him, she locked the door of the gallery and headed toward her favorite lunch destination, The Hungarian Tea Room. When in doubt, eat. She knew that she could not think this out sufficiently on an empty stomach.

Waiting for the Cobb salad and iced tea, Nora made the decision. The painting of Viburnum Gate hung on the wall over her roll top desk in the living room of her apartment. She looked at it often. It had affirmed her decision to follow her heart in dealing with the Nantucket house. Almost. But now, sitting in a sunny window, with wonderful food smells coming out of the kitchen, nothing seemed as important as keeping Viburnum Gate. She would keep it and take her chances that she could find work on the island. There had to be a change of hands when gallery managers left and openings appeared. Once she put her name around at the galleries, there would be a wait, of course. However she did have the small nest egg Aunt Bessie had left her. And, the summer rental income on the cottage out at Sconset was sizable.

For the next weeks, as the summer passed into a glorious fall, she hoped she might get back to the island by mid-September. Without discussing it with the owner, she had hired an assistant who was proving to be more than capable of covering for her while she took a few days off for a trip to the island. A first step. She could leave then because there would be a long-term show hanging. On loan from a prominent Boston family, the hugely popular show meant no changes would be necessary until mid-

October. Her new assistant could easily hold down the fort for a week or so. In fact, she was grooming Samantha Crocker for her job when she left to move permanently to Nantucket.

A brush-by hurricane a few days previous had left Nantucket Sound pretty disturbed on the day of her crossing. This time, she was completely oblivious to the other passengers. There might have been nothing but empty chairs around her, for all the attention she paid the other travelers.

She walked up Main Street from Straight Wharf despite the strong wind and rain the storm had left behind that would only weaken after all the hurricane's effects on the troubled ocean subsided. She arrived drenched at Viburnum Gate. It didn't matter, she was bubbling over with delight. The caretaker had watered the geraniums in the front windows and repaired two broken posts on the back porch.

She headed straight to the kitchen phone and punched in the number of the Martin House Inn. Melanctha answered. "Yes, of course I remember you Nora. On the island, are you?"

"Yes. Just wanted to say hello to Max. Is he there?"

"No, he's over in America picking up some supplies. Man saves money for the owner by picking the stuff up in his truck rather than having it shipped over. Wish the owner fully appreciated all the stuff that man does to cut costs. When he has his own place, his savvy habits picked up working for others will put him in good stead."

"Is he any closer to putting together a consortium, Melanctha?"

"I do believe it might be coming together. But you will have to ask him. I don't mix in his affairs."

Nora said goodbye saying she'd try calling Max the next day.

She changed into dry clothes and, pleased to see that the sun was working hard to come through the clouds, headed to the library.

"Hello, child. Welcome home. Staying for a while, Nora?"

"Hope so. Some last minute arrangements and I just might be moving in. Mabel, if you have the time, I have something I need to discuss with you…about Max."

An hour later, sitting with Mabel in her office, she had told her story about the possible family connection she and Max might share. "Bloodlines are interesting things in history," Mabel said, tapping her fingers on a large leather bound tome in front of her.

"At times, as you know from studying history, royal lines screwed themselves up badly by intermarrying. Didn't want to let any *common* blood into the line. Hillbillys produce idiots by marrying far too close, as well. Royal idiots and red neck idiots, don't know which is worse." She laughed. Nora wasn't sure where that left her and Max in this discussion.

"Should I tell Max or just forget all about it, Mabel."

Mabel looked out the window at the oak tree that had already gone rusty after a summer of green. "Guess you have to be honest with him, Nora. Although, from what you've told me, if it turns out that a line of Lauras with Maxwell bloodlines finally produced our Max, that doesn't necessarily mean that you two would turn out knuckle heads."

"You mean, if we married and had children, right?"

"Is that what you want, Nora?"

"Oh, Mabel, don't ask me that. First, let me deal with telling Max what I've learned."

The next day, Nora called Max and he sounded very pleased to hear from her. *May as well just get to it*, she told herself. *If we have any chance at all it won't be until this interesting little fact is out of the way. Or not.*

"I'm going to keep the house, Max. Just going to jump in over my head and hope I pop up and manage to swim."

"That's great. What better reason for a celebration? How about having dinner with me at Languedoc? Do you like French food?"

"Love it. Great idea. One of my favorite restaurants. How's tomorrow night? Let me take you, I'm the visitor."

"Not anymore. I insist this is my treat. I'll make a reservation for seven. It's halfway for each of us. Meet you there, okay?"

"I love walking to everything. I have a feeling my car is going to do a lot of sitting in the garage."

She brought with her a great, long, narrow, wine colored silky jersey dress with spaghetti straps, a sort of ankle length tank top that outlined every curve in her body. It made her feel scandalous. Not the kind of thing she usually gravitated to, although when she saw it at Filenes, she decided to try on a new persona. Max did bring out physical reactions in her that no one ever had sparked, previously.

Even though it was September, officially fall, it was still summery and, ignoring her Aunt Bessie's dictum that one must never wear white after Labor Day, she slipped into white leather sandals and pulled on a wide, white bone bracelet that had been Aunt Bessie's brought back from a trip to Africa.

Checking herself in the tall hall mirror, she noticed that the few days she'd grabbed to sit in the sun still showed in the blonde streaks in her light brown hair.

As she headed out the door, she realized that once the sun went down it would turn chilly. She returned to pull a long wine, white and cobalt blue paisley shawl from the hall closet.

What she had to do scared her because it might forever close the door on her potential relationship with Max. He might recoil. There was no way to know what his reaction would be.

Just as she was pulling the front door closed, the phone rang. She considered not answering. The cautious Nora could not ignore what might be an important call. So much for her transition to careless, insouciant, femme fatale.

"Hello."

"Oh Nora dear, is that really you? I was so afraid I'd missed you."

"Mabel, hi, what's up?"

"Well dear, I've been thinking. I know I told you that honesty is always the best policy but, well, I've had a change of heart."

Nora's stomach clenched. She was going forth this night determined to be courageous, taking Mabel's sage advice that she must tell Max the truth and not leave any doors open for mistakes to creep in. Was Mabel about to cut her off at the knees?

"Trust me, dear. I'm an old lady who sometimes goes all foggy in the noggin' however, how about if you simply put it off for awhile. I mean, don't overwhelm the boy with this news. Let's talk again about it. I talked to my pal Adele and she said that we might be able to untangle this because…Shush Bruno, Mommy's on the phone. Hey, got to go, Nora, time to feed the hound."

Nora could hear Mabel's wolfhound in the background and he sounded hungry and impatient. She had no choice; all her gathered courage for announcing that the two of them were cousins just dematerialized into vapor. She did trust Mabel and yet, she was so ready to get it over with and then move on. Of course, she was kidding herself about the moving on but it felt good standing there in that scrumptious dress feeling so empowered.

She pulled the front door closed and headed down toward Center Street. Turning the corner onto Center, not expecting to see him until she turned onto Broad, suddenly he materialized before her.

He was half a block away. He waved. She waved back. Her stomach lurched but she reminded herself that regardless of what Mabel said, Aunt Bessie would disagree. One does not mess around with relatives even if they are distant relatives. *It is simply not done.* She could hear her aunt's voice, always so sure of what is done and what is not done.

As their steps along the brick sidewalk brought them closer and closer, Nora imagined a door in her mind that was closing, closing, closed.

"I was early getting away so I came further along to meet you. Wow, you are a vision, Nora." With that, he pulled her arm through his and they walked along. She was aware of heads turning to look at them. She felt as if she was glowing like a bright candle.

An extraordinary dinner of seared tuna sitting under a mango chutney sauce, two bottles of costly French wine and chocolate covered strawberries in the flakiest, most buttery crust she'd ever tasted, left them both mellow. It occurred to Nora that the narrow dress might be stretched to the breaking point.

"How about coffee and a nightcap at Viburnum Gate, Max?" *Whoops, who said that?*

"Lovely. The walk will do us good. What a meal. What a wine. What a dessert."

Rising, taking her hand in his, he kissed it saying, "What a woman."

Nora gave herself permission to be the kind of woman who can enjoy a man without expecting a lifelong commitment. If she could have made a pact with the devil, she knew that she'd have traded one night with Max with no long term commitment against no night with Max. Why the hell not?

The house was warm and smelled of the lavender she'd placed in every room. Another fragrance, so redolent of childhood memories, was the sandalwood cupboard her aunt had brought back from India. Warm weather always brought out its exotic fragrance.

"I have crème de menthe and Frangelico, and something without a label that's in a nice, fancy bottle that looks like an after dinner drink, if you are daring." Nora laughed, thoroughly enjoying her own little quip and realizing that *she* felt liquid, languid and totally relaxed. She felt beautiful and daring. She was ready for Max.

Max moved over to the sideboard where she was lining up bottles. He turned her toward him and kissed her forehead. She moaned a low moan. Then, he kissed both ears, his breath tickling in a way that, although there was nothing funny about how it made her feel, she let out a little giggle. Next, it was her neck and then her chest while he removed the straps of her dress from her shoulders. By this time, Nora was so melted in the knees she grabbed onto Max for support, fearful she might just melt onto the newly sanded, shiny pine floor.

Leading her by the hand up the old pine stairs, he stopped at the top landing looking to her for direction. He had never been upstairs in the house and had no idea which room was hers. So she took the lead and directed him into her bedroom, formerly Aunt Bessie's, silently asking her dead aunt to forgive her for being so loose a woman. *Well, at least*, she said to her aunt, in absentia, *I am not letting a good opportunity get away. I am being an independent woman. You taught me to take matters into my own hands and not settle for less than I deserve. Here goes!*

The long dress slid down like cream over pudding and she removed Max's light blue cotton shirt and kissed his chest. She hadn't ever actually imagined his chest in detail although she had imagined him on top of her in bed. She liked what she saw, tanned, just slightly hairy, strong, and he smelled so good. That combination of simple soap and water, she thought it was Irish Mist soap, and just a hint of cologne or aftershave that again reminded her of Old Spice, but lemony.

When Max moved into her, she moaned loudly. She knew she should feel embarrassed for making such a loud noise, but she didn't. Because Max's moan matched her own in intensity and volume, she stopped worrying about such things. Like coming home, slowly he made love to her, kissing her mouth, her neck, her breasts, as he moved gently but determinedly inside her. When she felt it beginning she wondered for a second what was happening to her and then she knew that, although she wasn't terribly sexually experienced she might have misplaced the blame she'd put on herself; assuming she might be slightly frigid.

Never before had fate brought her the right man. Now she was truly a woman and there was no turning back. How could she ever again make love to a man who did not make her feel this way?

They slept for about an hour afterwards with Max wrapped around her with his head on her shoulder. She did not want to sleep. She wanted to savor. However, she soon slid into a gentle, sweet sleep safe in Max's arms. When they awoke they made love again and finally, at about four, Max declared that although it was the last thing he wanted to do, he had to go home to make bread and scones and coffee for fifteen guests.

"Sleep lovely one, dream about me. I'll bring you warm, buttery scones with strawberry jam and hot coffee in about six hours. Can you last?"

"I can last without the food, though it sounds scrumptious and I'm sure I'll devour it, but I won't last without you. Hurry back. With luck, I'll sleep till then and it will seem as if you came right back."

Max kissed her forehead and pulled the covers up to her neck. He slipped into his clothes and out the door. She would not see him again for many months.

ELEVEN

The answering machine was on the first floor and the phone had been turned off in the bedroom. When Max called at nine-thirty, Nora did not hear his anxious voice leaving her the message that would be all she'd hear from him for what seemed like an eternity. Never had she slept so deeply, so unaware of everything including the call that would change her life.

At nine-forty, awakening with a start, she jumped up and headed for the shower. She would be fresh and ready when he arrived with breakfast. The night before had been magical and she was still caught in its glow. The glow dissipated as time passed and no Max. At ten forty-five, she put down the book she'd become engrossed in as she waited. One look at the clock and she knew something had gone wrong. Max had been cornered by an inn guest or encountered a problem like a leaky faucet that required his immediate attention.

She started a pot of coffee and went searching in the refrigerator for something to eat. She'd have to do a real shopping for her stay, if she was going to eat in. The red light on the answering machine caught her attention. Oh good, Max's reason for not returning with freshly baked breakfast treats. The message wiped out her appetite completely.

"Nora, I have to fly to Puerto Rico right away. Got a flight off the island connecting with a flight leaving Boston at noon. My daughter has been in an accident. She is in critical care. Got to go. God, she just has to make it. Talk to you when I can."

For the rest of her stay, she waited to hear from Max but he did not call. She walked over to the inn every day to talk to Melanctha who also had no word from Max.

"I don't suppose he left you with a number where I could reach him in Puerto Rico?"

"No, he rushed out of here as soon as he got the call. I had just come in to start the breads when the call came. I just hope his daughter is all right. He loves that kid more than life itself. I promise I'll call you, if and when he calls me."

Nora walked around town, up and down streets and in and out of shops, unaware of people she passed, for two days. Ostensibly shopping for things for the house, but barely aware of the process, she finally pulled herself up short.

She needed to know how Max's daughter was doing and how Max was doing. But if he didn't want to ease her or Melanctha's worries then she had no choice but to get on with her own life. The decision to keep the house entailed lots of peripheral decisions like finding a job on the island and giving her notice in Boston.

The latter, surprisingly, was solved for her by a phone call from her employer. He had made a decision to close the Newbury Street gallery and retire to France. She was suddenly unemployed although he gave her a severance package of three month's salary. Three months to find a new job in a seasonal environment with lots of galleries that were, unfortunately for her, already being capably managed.

She and Bill Macy grew closer as Nora settled in to live permanently on her beloved island. With Max out of the picture, and no one the wiser as to when he would return, Nora turned to Bill for his quiet strength and guidance. She was unaware of Bill's falling in love with her. For Nora, he was the brother she'd never had.

When Nora called Marsha to tell her about Max's disappearance, she also told her about their one magnificent night of love.

"Be grateful for little delights, sweetie. Life is short and love is hard to find. Treasure that special night, few ever have anything close to that." She loved Marsha and counted on her for sisterly advice, but somehow this time it was just not enough. She wanted more. She wanted Max forever.

Christmas was melancholy that year as it had been the previous year, just after her aunt had died. Max's friends invited her to spend Christmas dinner with them at the Jared Coffin House and she accepted. They were all great people, bright, interesting and fun to be with, however, without Max there was something so obviously missing that did not escape any of them. They talked about Max, concerned about his daughter, but no one had heard from him. It was going on four months and Nora was beginning to feel as if she'd dreamed him.

On New Year's Eve, she joined Bill for dinner at La Languedoc, and it was pleasant, as always. Bill was full of old Nantucket stories that she enjoyed. His family went back as far her hers but he had spent a lifetime delving into the history that she had only dipped into on the surface.

After dinner, the night being windless and starry, they walked down to the waterfront. There were other strollers on Old South Wharf admiring the boats decorated with lighted trees on their bows or little fairy lights outlining ports and running up masts.

Bill took Nora's gloved hand and began to say something that she missed, her mind flown to thoughts of Max and how she wished he would return soon, in the new year.

When she brought up Max, she saw the look in Bill's eyes and suddenly realized that he was feeling something for her that she did not feel for him. Almost visibly, he stored away what he'd been about to say.

"I am sure that what is happening to his daughter is all he can handle right now, however the consortium he managed to pull together to buy the inn is demanding immediate attention. They have been patient and understanding as long as they could and it is time for Max to come back and deal with this urgent matter. Max could lose everything he has worked so hard to build here. I'm handling the legal end of the deal and the financial backers Max put together to buy the inn with him as CEO, for want of a better term, are confused and ready to pull out. Without Max at the helm, the whole thing threatens to crumble and fall. In fact, Melanctha told me on the QT that the owners have been meeting with another party interested in buying the place."

"Oh, Bill that would just destroy Max. Owning his own inn is everything he's ever dreamed about. What can we do?"

"Well the situation may reach critical mass, soon. This could be the end of his dream. I know for sure that the investors do not want to proceed without Max. He alone can make it work as planned. This kind of business is all about personality and the kind of people skills that Max has in spades."

They walked quietly side by side as the wind picked up and a light snow began to fall.

"Nora, don't let this change the quality of our friendship, but if Max were not in the picture, I would, as the young people say, put the moves on you. That said, I shall never mention it again."

Nora gave him a big hug and kissed him on the cheek. "Deal. But thanks. If I hadn't fallen for Max you would be the man I want to put the moves on me, Bill."

The two friends laughed and continued on their stroll as the gentle snow dusted their hats and coats.

Sitting over hot cider back at Nora's house, with a blazing fire and soft music in the background, Bill suggested a possible plan for locating Max.

"Nora, we do have a clue as to Max's whereabouts we can follow up on."

"Right. He is on Puerto Rico. I hear it is a pretty big island, Bill."

"Not so fast, woman. Hear me out. We know that his ex-wife runs a large hotel. We also know that his daughter was in hospital recently, hopefully not still. I have the power to check on such things. We know both his ex-wife's name and his daughter's. I would have thought of this sooner except that, until the backers started getting antsy, my only reason for finding Max was to ease your worries. Please forgive my selfishness, Nora."

"No need. All's well that ends well...at least, according to Aunt Bessie, the optimist. How long do you think it will take you to find him?"

"Give me a couple of days. I'll call you as soon as I know something."

TWELVE

"Happy New Year, dear Nora. Let's hope it is a better one worldwide as well as on our captured-in-amber island. Oh, I forgot to mention something important. Gerald Wentworth asked me to ask you to call him. He lost your phone number. He's a serious art connoisseur, but a bit scatterbrained. He could use someone organized like you to run things."

"I spoke to him last week. You mean he has a job for me?"

"I'd say so. He's off to Fiji soon and his manager just up and left to run off with a waiter at the Boarding House. Two positions suddenly opened up. Choose one."

"Let's see, eeny-meeny."

Kissing Nora's cheek and squeezing her arm, Bill wished her good luck. "It's the best gallery in town, but you will make it even better. Good night, dear friend."

As Nora was applying a bright green facial mask to her scrubbed face, considering what a great Halloween disguise it would make, the phone rang. She raced for it just as his voice came on like honey pouring into her heart.

"Sorry you are not there Nora, I…"

She grabbed the phone breathless and happy. "Max, it's me. I'm here. Hi, how are you, where are you, how is Jennie?"

"One question at a time, Nora." Max's voice held a smile. That smile that melted her heart and could light up a room. "Sorry, it's been so long. Jennie is just recently out of a coma and ready for lots of physical therapy."

"Oh, Max I had no idea. No one had any way of knowing what was happening to her. Or you. Everyone on the island has been worried. Did Bill find you?"

"Yes, like Sherlock Holmes, he called around the island and finally reached Miranda at the hotel. I know I should have called you and Melanctha and lots of people. I guess it seems pretty irresponsible and disinterested especially with regard to the inn situation. I have just been so focused on Jennie…I know everyone has grounds for being really pissed off, but I just haven't thought about anything but my daughter. It has been a perpetual nightmare. It was only yesterday that she awoke with no permanent brain damage. The doctors scared the hell out of us with the possibilities of what she might be like if she ever did wake up. I didn't even know that weeks and months had passed. I know that sounds like a lame excuse but it *has* been a blur. I've lived in her room in ICU. Learned to be a damned good nurse and just ate when someone told me to and slept in short naps so I could be guaranteed of being there when Jennie awoke and that is that."

His breath seemed to run out with his last word. He'd said so much, melted away her worries and gladdened her heart. He had called her. He cared.

"Oh Max, I've never been a parent, but I think I know how it must have been for you. No, no one is pissed at you. More like deeply concerned and wondering how we could help. Melanctha has been wonderful, running the inn and holding off the Visigoths." Nora laughed with relief and a sense of being in a drama that was now coming to a satisfactory conclusion.

"Bill has been terrific, he figured out how to track you down. The backers are meeting with him soon, maybe already, he hasn't called me to report, but he will. Did he tell you about all that?"

"Yes, he's been great. He met with them last week and he told me to tell you what transpired because he has laryngitis and I could barely make out what he was saying. Said he got a cold walking New Year's Eve. Everyone has been placated for the time being. The owners are still willing to consider our offer. Their other offer fell through anyway, so we are presently the only game in town."

"That's terrific. Can you talk for a bit more? Or are you in a hurry to get back to Jennie?"

"I *can* talk. It's so good to hear your voice. I've been listening exclusively to strange beeping and buzzing and ticking machines for ages. You and Bill are my only contact with the island right now and I'm feeling homesick. This one is nice, the weather is great, in the eighties, but I really miss our island."

Nora did not fail to hear the "our" and wondered if she was being presumptuous in assuming he meant hers and his and not an editorial "our" that included all the residents of Nantucket.

"What does your schedule look like now that Jennie is improving?"

"Well, there is a long road still ahead. The doctors think she will walk again but not before months of physical therapy. Right now, because of all the drugs, she is feeling pretty down and discouraged. I have to instill in her a lot of positive attitude and they tell me that once they get her drugs down to maintenance level, she will start to focus on getting better. Damned drugs. Sure they help some things to heal but they affect the mind so that the patient is low and vulnerable and depressed. I will be here to help her all the way. Miranda has been wonderful, of course. She has a demanding job but she is here whenever she can get away. Together we are working to get our Jennie back."

"We." Nora wondered how much of a new we they had become. She knew that many broken families had been pulled back together, tighter than ever, over a shared child's misfortune.

"If you have the time I'd like to tell you about my new job and my research into Simon Graystone's life, remember, our little-known artist?"

"Nora...your voice sounds so great, I could talk all night, not that I can but, thanks for being there and helping with everything in my absence." He sounded tired but still willing to listen.

"Gerald Wentworth hired me to run his gallery, Wentworth & Wentworth. It was his and his father's but he inherited it and has little interest except in the income department. I love it. He's just about moved permanently to Fiji and given me carte blanche."

"Congrats. That's terrific. So, you can be a full-time islander now, Nora."

"Looks that way. What I want to do is find as many of Simon Graystone's pieces as I can. It will take time and a lot of research combined with advertising to seek out people who might remember owning one and storing it away in the attic. Gerald has approved a large advertising budget and the Artists Association is working with me."

"Swell."

"Max, are you ready for some peripheral information I uncovered that involves your family roots?" In for a penny, in for a pound. Mabel had verified that there would be no danger in their, as she put it, "swapping genetic material" because of the distance of the relationship.

"What? How could you have done that? I mean, what the heck are you talking about, Nora?"

"Bear with me. Remember the story Mabel told us about the Laura in Aunt Bessie's family who gave birth to an illegitimate child and was taken in by my family? Well, her family too."

"Sure."

"Well, later Laura turned up after she put the child up for adoption. That child grew up in a happy home in a tiny town called Barre, in the middle of Massachusetts."

"Hang on. My mother came from there."

"I know; that's the whole point. Your grandmother was Laura's adopted child and your mother, Laura, according to my research, married John Henry Michelson and they bore a son who was named for an old family name, Maxwell."

"So, let me get this straight, the adopted child knew her father was that Maxwell sailor guy who dumped the original Laura."

"Seems that the first Laura insisted that the child be told who her real father was. She did make him out, according to the family, to be quite a naval hero who died with honors in battle."

"Wow. Will wonders never cease? That's a lot to think about, isn't it?"

"I'm sorry if the timing is not so good. Maybe I should have waited until you return to the island." She waited for him to say that he'd be returning soon but he didn't.

"You do realize that makes us related, don't you. Well, of course you do."

"Mabel checked all the information I discovered and she says that we are so distantly related that it would never be a concern if we..."

Silence.

"Got to go. Doctor wants to speak to me, Nora. I promise to call once a week and as soon as Bill has all the nitty-gritty pulled together, I will fly home. With any luck, I might bring Jennie with me."

Left unsaid was whether Miranda might come along, as well. Nora had to keep her mind from focusing on this possibility or it would drive her mad.

Max called one week later, to the day. His news uprooted all of Nora's well-planted and cherished positive hopes.

"I moved into Miranda's house because the hospital got sick of seeing me walking the halls and sleeping on stairs and benches. Today however, Jennie came home. We've got a lot to do now but we are elated, and I am finally rested."

What could Nora do but tell him that she was happy things were progressing so well? Inside her head, she conjured scenes of the reunited couple sharing a bed making love in the cooling easterly breezes of the Caribbean island.

She placed two ads, one in the *Nantucket Inquirer Mirror*, affectionately called the *Inky*, and one in the *Boston Globe*. She was offering a free art appraisal day for any works from sketches to paintings or even letters written by Simon Graystone. Her good friend Abram agreed to come over the help her with the project. "Of course, you know Abram, we may not see a single piece of work. Anyway, I promise you a great lunch at the restaurant of your choice."

The interview she gave the *Inky* reporter did bring people into the gallery out of curiosity. Before long, she had set in motion a scavenger hunt that would not only be fun for those doing the hunting but would, hopefully, help her to make her mark on the island art scene.

Abram called two days after the ad in the Boston paper with news of a man in Denver who had a Graystone.

"The man says his grandparents stayed here years ago and bought a painting of Brant Point Light right from the painter. It is a signed Graystone, Nora. That makes two."

"Thanks, Abe. Is he willing to loan it?"

"Yes, his lawyer is drawing up the papers as we speak."

Abram's fax number had been included in the ad as the appraiser.

She hung up the phone and it rang immediately. It was Abram. "Two more paintings have been found in California and the owner wants to sell them if the appraisal is appealing."

Twenty minutes later, Nora picked up the phone. "Me again. Two emails and one phone call so our collection is growing rapidly. A woman from California called to say that her parents honeymooned on the island in nineteen twenty-eight and they bought a small canvas for six dollars, from a young man who biked all over the island painting. Another woman from Chicago called to say that she has hanging on her wall a large canvas entitled, on the back, The Nantucket Moors. And guess who signed it?"

"Oh Abe, this is amazing."

"What is really amazing is how many people formerly from Boston or with ties here read the *Globe* on-line. Lucky for us."

By the time Nora was ready to close up the gallery that night, Abram had called again.

"Hold your breath Nora, got an email from a woman right here in Boston telling me that she has four Graystones and one that looks like his but the signature is missing along with a large section of the paint. She says it was in a fire and received some water damage. However, I am on my way right now to look at her collection. She is very interested in selling. Will your budget stretch to cover all of these works by a painter who may or may not inspire a new interest in his work?"

"The art market is like a curious gourmand anxious to taste its next new palette-pleasing dish. The true art lovers, the collectors, as opposed to those who purchase a painting because the turquoise in the sky matches exactly the turquoise in the fabric on their living room couch, are just waiting to discover someone new. I've been in contact with Mr. Wentworth, the owner, and he will provide enough money to purchase anything that does not sell as a result of the retrospective. Nothing like a long dead artist to spark new interest, Abe."

Just as Nora was walking out the door of the gallery, the phone rang again. *If it's Abe he can call me at home. It's been a long day, I want my dinner.* She almost let the machine get the call. Then, she turned and headed to the desk.

The spidery voice on the other end announced herself as, "Hello, Adele Macy Lombard, ancient monument, calling to speak to the new art lady, please."

"Hello Ms. Lombard, Nora Kavanagh speaking. I guess that would be me, the new gallery director."

"Oh yes my dear, how nice. Yes, yes, I've just been speaking to that dear boy, Bill Macy, a distant cousin." Her voice seemed to wake up and grow stronger as she spoke. As if she did not speak often, but once started, got better at the infrequent act.

"Well, he instructed me to call and speak to you. You see, I finally gave in and decided that I am too old to keep secrets anymore. Bill assured me that you would not only respect my secrets, but make good use of them."

Nora smiled, trying not to sound as if she was making light of this strange conversation, she said, "If Bill says so, I am flattered that he has given me such a high recommendation. I certainly would hope to respect whatever it is you wish to share with me Mrs. Lombard."

"Never mind the Mrs. I am not a married lady. I am rather, a woman of experience and passion who chose not to squander her talents on only one man. Always had enough passion to spread around. In fact, it is about that passion that I am now ready to spill the beans. Come to tea here. I am way out at Wauwinet, next door to the inn. Just follow the road until just before the inn and turn left onto my dirt lane. There is a little sign there that says, Wildwood Lane. My house is Wildwood. Isn't it nice how we name our houses here? Some people from away think it is odd but I say, love your pets, name them, love your children, name them, love your boats, name them, and for heavens sake, why not a beloved house? Tenish tomorrow, alrighty dear?" She hung up and Nora sat looking at the phone.

Down at the waterfront, in the old former brick warehouse built by his forbearers, Bill Macy hung up the phone and realized that he had just taken on a Cupid role, unwittingly.

When Max called him at nine a.m., he was full of good news. Jennie was walking and her spirits were up. She was full of the determination to succeed and get back to her active teenage life. Bill was delighted and told Max so, extending his good wishes to this child he had never met but who had come to be cared about by the many islanders who cared about Max. Bill hadn't yet found the time to tell Nora but he had told Max that a date and time had been set to sign the purchase papers.

"Hi, Bill, I've booked a flight for tomorrow. I'll get to the island around two. I'll come from the airport directly to your office so we can look things over before the Thursday signing."

"Excellent, I shall look forward to seeing you. I was just about to call Nora. Shall I tell her?"

"If you wouldn't mind, no. I'd like to surprise her. Sorry if this sounds like a lovesick teenager but I am feeling like one, so here goes. I'd like you to invite her to lunch on Thursday but don't tell her that I'll be there. If we get things all ready to go tomorrow for the four o'clock meeting on Thursday, we will have time for lunch at the Atlantic prior to the meeting. Make it sound like it will be just the two of you. She and I have been talking regularly on the phone but I haven't mentioned when I'd be home. Do you mind, Bill?"

Polite Bill assured Max that he'd be happy to set up the surprise lunch date, but his heart wasn't really in it.

Finally, it was time for Nora's meeting with Adele Macy Lombard.

She and Mabel and Aunt Bessie had all been close friends and all shared secret crushes on Simon Graystone. But, had one of them shared more than a crush with the artist, she wondered? Mabel had hinted at something scandalous or at least, something secret that she had sworn to keep to herself that was linked to Adele.

Being a stickler for punctuality, Nora arrived at Adele's a little early. The house, more than a cottage but less than a house like graced the streets of town, was natural shingled with tall windows and lots of lovely gardens surrounding it. Gardens in which someone, maybe Adele, maybe a clever hired gardener, had succeeded in getting things to grow out of sand. She supposed a lot of mulch and top soil had been added but, just the same, this stretch, where Coatue began, was nothing but sand and some saw grass.

Wildwood was imposing. Although not that large, it was the wraparound porch and three stories that gave it a look of not only strength against the punishing winds coming at it much of the year, but also, a certain look of pride of place.

A typical Nantucket turn of the century summer place built when architects loved adding copious gables and turrets, the house was a smaller version but still as fanciful as any mansion of its style. Victorian to the last board.

Adele welcomed her with a smile. Saying not a word, the old woman led Nora, cane tapping on the shiny wide pine boards of the hallway, to the back veranda overlooking the shining azure waters of the Head of the Harbor.

Framed by the expanse of windows sat a British high tea complete with tiered cake server, silver teapot and dainty porcelain cups and plates.

"I'll pour, dear, and you can just dig in. I employ a French pastry chef, retired and at my beck and call. That is why the wide girth beneath this tent of a dress."

Nora immediately liked Adele. "Is this really real clotted cream, Miss Lombard?"

"Yes, I have it imported and please, it is just Adele. Anything else makes me feel old." The smile was not old at all. Nora noticed that although Adele had some deep wrinkles her eyes were full of youth and what looked like little devils just waiting to burst onto the scene. She'd never before seen eyes that, as described in books, *twinkled,* but this woman's eyes most certainly did just that.

"I hope you like a nice, traditional British cream tea dear. I have one every day. Bring the clotted cream in special on an airplane. Isn't it just magnificent, and kind of impossible to believe how one can get what one wants from anywhere these days? Have some of that magnificent strawberry jam, my neighbor makes it from my strawberries and it is ambrosial."

Nora settled into the comfortable white wicker chair's blue and yellow chintz cushions and nearly drooled. Adele poured the tea and held the cream pitcher up, silently asking if Nora wanted it in her tea. Nora shook her head. Adele held the sugar tongs over the bowl and Nora asked for just one cube. She felt as if she'd slipped into a British mystery. The mystery was, however, not who murdered the duke in the parlor, but what did this woman know about Simon Graystone.

After an hour of chatting about the island, during which Adele told her many stories of the "old days" when she was growing up there, she suddenly said, "Well, now for the piece de resistance. I know you and Gerald are cooking up a nice plan to show off our romantic artist Simon Graystone. Mind you, I would call him a romantic in more ways than one. His work was soft, gentle, filled with the beauty of place *and* he was also a very romantic man. A passionate man."

"Did you know him well, Adele?" Might as well jump in and get to the meat of it all, Nora told herself.

"Some might call him a heart breaker, a Lothario, a gigolo. Not I. What must be understood, child, is that it is the men who do *not* break our hearts, those who remain and grow boring, who are soon forgotten. We never forget the heartbreakers."

Well, it was difficult to come up with a comeback on that one, although Nora tried. Instead, she simply smiled and Adele continued.

"Simon broke my heart but, *c'est la vie.* 'Better to have loved and lost than never to have loved at all.' At least he did not leave me with a bambino…just a broken heart, soon mended. He was the only man who just might have netted me. I, however, was not first in line."

Then, her voice lower, looking around as if someone might be listening, she added. "In my attic I have about thirty-six or seven paintings done by my beloved Simon. He left them in my care just before he jumped from the eleventh floor of the hotel where we had a cozy apartment in wonderful, Bohemian Greenwich Village. My money, of course, paid the rent."

Nora wondered if the look of astonishment on her face was as overwhelming to Adele as it was to her. She was speechless with delight and fascination.

"You have an attic full of Graystone paintings?"

"Yes. And I am willing to share him. I was not so willing, years ago, when he wanted your Aunt Bessie. I suppose that I have mellowed over the years."

THIRTEEN

"Hi Deidre. I'm meeting Bill for lunch, is he here yet?"

The hostess at the Atlantic Café smiled and motioned toward the table in the corner right by the front window. As Nora looked in that direction, she saw Bill and he waved. The man whose head was back to her did not move. He was not alone. Her heart did a neat flip. The ponytail was gone, but she knew who it was and her knees did what all the romance novels say that knees do when you see someone who makes your heart race. Max.

Trying with all her might to control her jellied legs, she walked slowly toward the table. Just as she got there, Max turned and smiled. When she thought about it later, once her breathing normalized, she wondered how she managed to stand dignified when she wanted to throw her arms around him and ravish him right there in front of God and everyone.

"Hi Nora. Bet you never expected to find me here. Don't be mad at good old Bill, I threatened him with exposure if he told you. You see, I just happen to know that as a kid he used to take his catboat over to Coatue and shellfish without a license."

Bill guffawed and put his hand to his forehead and rolled his eyes as if to indicate that he was cornered and the truth was finally coming out.

Good old Max, Nora thought, always open with a joke and keep 'em laughing. Max pulled out a chair next to him and she sat. The conversation was mostly directed by Max. He filled them in on Jennie's progress, how much he disliked the constant perfect weather of Puerto Rico and how wonderful his ex-wife, Miranda, had been through all the difficult times. She hoped that Adele's jaded view of love and marriage turned out to be dead wrong. She didn't think that she'd be as good about spending the rest of her life mooning over the joy of having received a broken heart from a man she'd adored.

Soon after Bill's last mouthful of clam chowder and corn bread, his favorite lunch, he excused himself saying he had an urgent appointment. Bill reminded Max of the four o'clock meeting and off he went.

Alone with Max, feeling a little more relaxed having had a glass of red wine with her lunch, Nora asked him how long he planned to be on-island.

"I have to sign the papers and reassure the backers and then fly back to get Jennie. She had too many things to clean up before she could come with me. I just hope Miranda doesn't manage to talk her out of her decision."

"So, Jennie will be living here on the island then."

"Looks that way. When I come back, finally, with Jennie, will I find you here and ready to take me back, Nora?"

"Odd question, isn't it, Max. Since you left suddenly, I've moved house and taken a job and am becoming a part of the island. I seem to be here to stay. I guess I have to ask you if you will want to pick up where we left off."

Max leaned over and kissed her mouth. Gently, barely touching, like being brushed by a moth's wings.

"If this were not a public place, I would show you how much I want to pick up just where we left off."

That was a good enough answer for her. "Tell you what, after your signing, I could make us some dinner at my house and you can remind me where we left off months ago."

Listening to herself she suddenly realized that she liked the way she sounded. She sounded like an interesting, attractive woman. Things had changed.

Max headed to Bill's office on Straight Wharf, and Nora raced to the A&P for dinner supplies. They barely touched the jumbo shrimp and pasta Nora had lovingly prepared. By the time they made it to Nora's bedroom, their clothes were scattered up the stairs like some Hansel and Gretel breadcrumb trail. When Nora's head hit the pillow and Max's warm breath closed in on her face, kissing her nose, her eyes, her ears, her forehead, back to her nose, and then gobbling up her mouth like a starving man, she was overwhelmed. She began to cry and Max kissed away her tears.

Max's hands caressed her body as if it was the first female body ever, his Eve. If she had to fight Miranda for this man, she was willing to take her on even if a mean serpent was involved.

Max flew back to Puerto Rico and Nora dedicated almost every hour to her plan for a Graystone retrospective. Adele called to tell her that if she wanted to inspect the cache in her attic, wearing "grubbies, because I don't send the cleaning lady up there. It's knee deep in dust, Nora."

On her knees, Nora did a cursory inspection of each painting. Later back at the gallery, she'd work with a magnifying glass, q-tips and diluted alcohol as she carefully cleaned them to bring up their original colors.

Adele was sipping afternoon tea on the back porch when Nora, dusty and wreathed in feathery cobwebs, came to report her finding.

"The grand total is thirty-seven." She choked on the number as she spoke it. This had been so far beyond her expectations when she began.

After wrapping the paintings carefully in bubble wrap and loading them into the van she'd inherited with the job, Nora headed back to town. It had been a wonderful day up until she picked up the phone in the gallery as she entered the back door.

"Hi, hon. Good and bad news."

"Oh, no, is Jennie still doing well?"

"Jennie is fine. That's the good news. She's excited about starting school on the island. Bad news is that Miranda has taken the job managing the Nantucket Inn out by the airport. Damn her. She never even consulted me. She decided she needs a change and with Jennie moving on with me, she's decided she can remain part of her life by being there. Believe me, I had not the slightest suspicion, or hint, that she was plotting this."

"She and Jennie are moving here permanently?" Nora could not believe what she was hearing. Finally, she was getting Max back, but he was coming back with a complicated package. She had been looking forward to meeting Jennie but Miranda too…

Reading her mind, Max interjected into her images of doom. "It won't affect us, Nora. You will love Jennie and she will get a better high school education here, better preparation for college. Now that I will own the inn, I will be able to afford her college expenses. Miranda will probably tire of the island in no time. She hates the cold. This is just a way for her to hang on, she is so afraid of losing Jennie. She came so close when we almost lost our daughter. Now, she is just reacting without properly thinking it through. Please believe me, this is not a problem for us."

Nora wanted to believe Max. He hadn't said the three magic words yet, but she did believe that he loved her and it was only a matter of time. They had a deep, trusting friendship, mutual respect for one another's careers and ambitions and well, if sexual harmony had a language all its own, this one was singing, yes, yes, yes, in melodic strains.

The retrospective plans rolled along smoothly. More smoothly than her personal life. Nora was happy to adopt the name Adele had supplied, ***Images Of The Gray Lady Then and Now.*** Nora put out the word that she was also interested in photos from the period when Simon Graystone painted on the island and she received hundreds. She decided to get school children involved by offering prizes for identifying the places in some of the collection that were not identified. Some things would have changed but many would look pretty much the same after all the decades that had passed. She suggested that they take current photos to compare to the unnamed paintings.

Nora loved that she had managed to get islanders of all ages involved. She had copies of each painting made at the copy shop for purposes of identification. It became a popular scavenger hunt.

Nora was so busy, putting in long hours at the gallery, talking to both townspeople and tourists, and comparing notes with Abram, who was busy coordinating from his office in Boston, she lost track of the days. Max called to say he was hoping to book a flight for the following week. What she did not know until it was too late was that he and Jennie and Miranda had taken an earlier flight. As Max settled Jennie in at the inn, planning to head to the gallery to surprise Nora, Miranda beat him to it.

Late on a Saturday afternoon that had turned cool, rain hanging in the dark clouds ready to dump its contents on the island, Nora's back was turned when she heard the gallery door open. She would be closing in a few minutes, but she never turned away a potential customer.

The voice was deep and quite lovely. "Goodness, it's so damned cold. I'd forgotten. I don't know how you can stand it this time of year. I guess my blood has thinned from living in Puerto Rico."

Nora turned so fast she almost lost her balance. There, standing in the doorway, her dark hair catching the overhead light causing red highlights to pop, was a petite but curvaceous woman dressed like a Romanian gypsy. Her haunting looks reminded Nora of old Biblical paintings. Salomé came to mind.

Nora started to speak but the woman cut her off. "I suppose you are Nora Kavanagh."

"Yes, welcome to the Gerald Wentworth Gallery. Enjoy yourself. Browse around. Let me know if you have any questions." She thought she'd managed to sound professional and in control despite her churning stomach. Maybe the woman would just take a quick look around and leave. She could only hope. Nora's utter confusion was compounded by wondering why Miranda had arrived earlier than Max.

"Hello, I am Miranda Fox." Miranda stepped forward, hand extended. "Max has spoken so kindly of you. He is very grateful for all the help you provided while he and I were caring for our daughter. Thankfully, the horror is over and we are all healthy, safe and together here. I just wish it would get warm. When *does* the warm weather start?"

Miranda's physical presence, deeply tanned skin and raven hair severely swept back into a knot on the back of her head and held in place with a large tortoise shell comb somehow filled the space with a murky dusky quality. Nora felt something heavy, a change in the air. Her presence conjured up in Nora's head images of gypsy wagons and tambourines and wild, gyrating dances. Yet, overlaid on these images she felt something else, something almost sinister.

She wasn't going to go away so Nora smiled and asked if Max had also come back. Miranda nodded her head and the large, shoulder-brushing, gold hoop earrings swung, catching the light. Both arms were lined with tinkling bangle bracelets of gold, silver, colorful beads and what looked to be tiny, snow white and pink seashells.

Nora, saved by the phone, excused herself and when she returned to the main showroom moments later, Miranda had vanished. Nora could feel the air change as soon as the woman left. She didn't believe in things like magic and conjurers affecting the atmosphere with spells, but she just might be willing to change her mind about such things. The woman emitted a sense of danger.

So, Max was back. He hadn't let her know because he was reunited with Miranda. From moment to moment, this relationship was subject to change. Could she, she asked herself, flex and bend sufficiently to survive the stress.

When Max arrived minutes later, she wondered if he and Miranda had come into town together. Was Miranda the advance guard?

"Sorry I didn't call. We were on standby and not expecting to leave so soon. Three seats freed up and we had to hustle. Then I lost my cell. I took Jennie to the inn and Melanctha is feeding her. All I wanted was to see you.

When he took her in his arms, all was well. Max never devised excuses to cover his tracks; he was always up-front. Nora had learned that, even when things appeared ambiguous, he always cleared them up with honesty and integrity.

She told him about the strange meeting. "I know this probably sounds odd but I actually felt threatened by her, Max. I can't explain it; she was an ominous presence. I don't think I invented my response just because I'd rather not have her on the island, I think she had black thoughts about me."

Max steered her into the back sitting room and pushed the louvered door halfway closed so that they could have some privacy. "Darling Nora, Miranda is Jennie's mother. She pushed it too far this time but I feel sure she won't last too long in this climate. The first frost and she's gone. She enjoys appearing to be a mysterious woman. She dresses and acts like some kind of mystic. It's just a façade. She is a good woman and a great mother. I'm sorry she did that to you."

Max's kisses set off a lovely arpeggio in her head and once again, she felt safe, secure and loved. Until Max arrived to kiss away the sense of gloom created by Miranda's insertion of dusk into an otherwise bright day, she had been asking herself how she could compete with a woman whose mere presence seemed shrouded in a darkling mist.

The following day, Max called to invite her to dinner with him and Jennie at Vincent's Italian restaurant. Nora wanted this initial meeting to go well. At least Miranda would not be there. She was curious as to which parent Jennie most resembled. She hoped it was not her mother.

Adele called just as she was about to close and lock the front door of the gallery, to head to Vincent's.

"I won't keep you but a minute, dear. I know you wanted to find a photo of Simon. I have been going through old trunks, Mabel is working with me as my knees don't bend and unbend so well these days. We found a bonanza I forgot I had. A nice, full album, that kind with heavy, black paper pages to which you attached those little white corners that grip the photos. Everything is in that old sepia tone. Used to make photos look like antiques even when they were brand new."

"Oh, that's wonderful, Adele. It will make such a difference if people can really relate to him through his photo. May I come out tomorrow to see them?"

FOURTEEN

"Why do they call the island The Gray Lady?" Jennie asked, looking around at the murals of ships, early island houses, whales and one entire wall depicting a Nantucket "sleigh ride."

"Because of the fog." Nora and Max answered simultaneously and all three laughed. Nora added, "I will accept that appellation however I've also been told that it is because of all the lovely grayed, natural shingle houses."

"Both are true. But we do excel in fog production. The island is sitting between the Atlantic and the Sound and, as meteorologists explain it, the dew point is easily reached, resulting in fog. That is the temperature at which the air can hold no more moisture, creating fog.

"I saw a t-shirt that said, *Fog happens*."

Max reached over and patted Jennie's cheek and she leaned into him until their foreheads touched. Nora had become aware of the similarity of their voices, their laughs and even their hand gestures. And, thankfully, she was the female version of Max; light haired, pale from her hospital stay but already gathering a procession of tiny freckles across her nose from walking all over town since her arrival.

She wanted Jennie to like her so that she could share her with Max and be part of a perfect triangle of love and affection. A family.

"You know, at home, I mean, in Puerto Rico, there is an ancient lady who lives outside the city, out where a lot of poor people live in run down shacks and she is called the gray lady, but in Spanish. She does voodoo. I guess people go to her for curses and charms, you know, strange stuff like that. Some of my friends really believe she can curse people and even cause them to die. But I didn't believe it. I wouldn't ever go near there again. I went once with Mom when she went to buy some dried fish. That woman was sitting on her front door step and she looked at me and her eyes were really weird, watery, like fish eyes. I wouldn't go with Mom after that. Yuck. Maybe she *could* curse people. Sure gives a different meaning to gray lady, huh?"

Max let the comment drop and switched Jennie's attention to the next course by handing her the dessert menu. "Dessert sweetie? I suggest you try our famous New England Indian Pudding. You love molasses and this is made with corn meal and molasses and it's scrumptious."

Max cleverly diverted Jennie from her long story but not before Nora felt a little shiver across her shoulders remembering Miranda's eyes. They had penetrated Nora's skull like a laser beam. What color were they? Strange, they seemed to be colorless or maybe pale gray like a winter pond on a sunless day. Voodoo. Something came in that door with Miranda, something dark and chilling. Nora was sure she had not imagined this. It was something palpable and threatening. Nora shook the memory away, not wanting to spoil the lovely evening with Max and Jennie.

After dinner, they walked around town, the evening being comfortable, although not warm, but they all had worn light jackets. Max bought the Fog Happens t-shirt for Jennie. Nora stepped into the kitchen shop on Center Street to buy a copper colander she saw in the window. The shops had reopened for evening foot traffic in anticipation of a busy summer season.

They headed back to Viburnum Gate and Nora showed Jennie the moongate. As much as Nora wanted to take Max up to her bed, it was more important for her to make sure that Jennie liked her and trusted her. She had an idea about something they might share that would be fun.

"Jennie, there has always been a cat at Viburnum Gate. My aunt died last year, her cat Moses died shortly before, and since then, there has been no cat. I think we need one, maybe two. Would you like to go with me to the shelter to choose a couple of kitties?"

"Oh, I'd love to, Nora. I love cats. When?"

"How about tomorrow?"

"How about ten in the morning?"

Leaving his daughter waiting in the car, Max, ostensibly to say something to Nora, Max nipped back inside. He kissed Nora and promised to return in about an hour.

He explained that he couldn't spend the night because of Jennie, so he slipped out when Nora fell off to sleep.

Nora's dream was lucid and terrifying. She was walking on a dirt road and it was very, very hot. Miranda, her face wildly painted and her hair sticking out in all directions, done up in dreadlocks, jumped out from behind a bush and threw Nora to the ground. She hissed in her ear that she must never go near *her* Max again. Then she stuck something into Nora's neck. It felt awful, like a long needle. When she pulled it out and stared into Nora's eyes, Nora could see that there was no color, her eyes were pellucid but from out of the center, the iris, shot flames that burned Nora's eyes.

She awoke screaming and rubbing at her eyes.

Groping for the bedside table and then the doorframe, she managed to nearly crawl to the bathroom to splash cold water into her burning eyes. She was ill in the toilet. Flipping on the light and looking into the mirror she expected to see horrible burning flesh, but there was nothing out of the ordinary staring back at her.

At the Nantucket Inn, Miranda's bedroom light was on late. The doll she'd formed from wax and hair pulled from Nora's hairbrush, was nearly finished. That afternoon, when she'd found that, like most trusting islanders, Nora had left the back door unlocked, she gathered what she needed. Miranda smiled as she gazed on the doll that also wore a cotton scarf that had been lying on Nora's bureau. It would not be long now. Max would be hers and Nora would be no more.

As Nora worked at the gallery the following day, she could not shake the sense that somehow, way beyond her belief system or imagination, Miranda had actually entered her dream and meant to harm her.

If only the temperature would drop to twenty below and snow fall in blizzard conditions. Maybe then, Miranda would flee back to the sunshine of her old life. Sure, fat chance in June.

Max came by just as she was locking up and he walked her home. They talked about Jennie's growing love of the island and the new friend she'd made at the soccer camp he'd enrolled her in. "I have to get back to the inn but I need a few minutes alone with you."

"I hope Jennie will grow t like me."

"She already does, love. I have to confess, although it's probably silly of me, a grown man, I'm a little shy about grabbing you and ravishing you in front of Jennie."

"Well, I would hope so." They laughed and kissed at Nora's back door. As she watched Max walk away, she felt something chilling emanating from her normally safe and happy house. Suddenly she wanted to call out, "Come back, something bad is here waiting for me." Knowing this was foolish, and he'd laugh at her, she bucked up her courage and headed inside.

Reaching for the doorknob in the dusk of the overhanging porch roof, Nora felt it and knew without seeing it clearly what it was. Miranda had worn one on her right arm. Nora remembered it because of the delicate pink and white shells, tropical shells.

It was actually quite lovely except for the fact that Nora knew that it was not meant as a friendship gift but something else. Something sinister. Tiny white shells with pink interiors, curled around with an edge of pale tan crimping where the outer edge stopped, leaving the pink, silky interior slightly exposed. They looked far too delicate to have been drilled in order to string them on the elastic band that held them together and made the bracelet into a one-size-fits-all piece of jewelry.

Not for a moment did she imagine that Miranda meant it as a friendly gift. She removed it from the doorknob and, holding it in her hand she wondered how such a lovely thing could send out such frightening vibes? Was she creating something out of nothing? *Much Ado About Nothing*? Had her own fear of the imagined competition that Miranda posed set in motion the strange, portentous feelings? Was she overreacting and going a bit off the grid like an unbalanced, immature and unreasonably jealous woman? Or was Miranda a serious *and* dangerous threat?

Nora sat in the dark of the screened porch gently moving on the glider feeling paralyzed with confusing impressions. The honeyed aroma of the vine that twisted up the porch posts, rather than smelling sweet, turned sour in her nose. A scent that always made her feel happy and safe was now cloying and deceptive, meant to lull her into a kind of trance wherein she would find Miranda waiting to harm her.

How far, Nora wondered, would Miranda go to keep Max for herself? Hours passed, the moon rose, and a chill off the Atlantic made her shiver, and still she sat.

Was that a shadow over by the cottonwood tree? Perhaps a trick of the moonlight.

Nora held her breath. If she did not make a sound, whatever it was, perhaps an animal or a teenager playing games with another teenager, would show itself. She was sure she couldn't be seen in the deep shadows of the porch. She could remember scooting in and out of backyards all the way up Main Street with her friend Pepper before so many newcomers put up fences to divide their properties from their neighbors'.

The shadow began to grow more solid as it came closer. The moonlight hadn't yet come around to illuminate the porch; she was still safe. She shivered and her heart beat a fast tattoo.

The figure wore a long skirt and bracelets jingled on her arms. Nora was holding the shell bracelet Miranda had left for her, a gift with strange portents. She couldn't see the other woman grab the door handle but she knew that was what she was doing. She would find her gift gone and assume that Nora was inside. Yet, there were no lights on. Would that discourage her and send her away? Nora shivered again considering what might happen next if she were inside. She never locked her back door. Nantucketers never did. No need…until now.

The woman, who Nora knew was Miranda, stopped and stepped back off the porch onto the brick walkway. She looked up toward Nora's bedroom window where a simple electric candlelight glowed on the windowsill.

Then she turned and moved away. A few steps down the brick path she partially turned and looked over her shoulder. Again, looking up, to where Nora would be sleeping if her troubling thoughts had not stayed her, obviously for hours. She carried the shell bracelet inside and stuffed it into a cubbyhole in the roll top desk in the kitchen. Then she turned and locked the back door.

FIFTEEN

Olivia, the high school teacher who had enthusiastically taken on the "scavenger hunt" of identifying locations Simon Graystone had painted, stepped into the gallery.

"Good morning Olivia, how nice of you to stop by." Nora always found Olivia's sunny enthusiasm a great pickup and just what she needed at that moment. She hadn't slept much after Miranda's surprise visit.

"Hi, Nora, I just want to thank you again for getting my classes involved in your art search. They just love it. They are all over the island trying to locate the Graystone painting locations. Parents have gotten involved. Families are making Saturday and Sunday family outings with the painting copies in hand. They are walking into marshes, around ponds and along the shore. It's just great."

"I'm so pleased Olivia. I was hoping it would be fun but it really took off way beyond my expectations."

Olivia stayed for a cup of tea and she commented on how helpful Jennie had been to her by volunteering to help with another summer art project that Olivia was running for elementary school children. "Jennie is such a nice, responsible kid. Sometimes she does say some strange things about her mother however. Odd. I'm never quite sure what she means. She seems to want to talk to someone and yet, she also seems afraid. I haven't pushed her but sometimes she starts to say something and then she pulls back. Hey, relationships between teenage girls and their mothers, God knows, are quagmires at best."

Olivia accepted a second cup of tea and she and Nora sat companionably until the bell on the gallery door jingled as it was opened by a customer. In came a dark cloud.

Olivia picked up her purse and thanked Nora for the tea, excusing herself saying she had to get on with her shopping. As she passed Miranda, who had only entered a few feet, the teacher said "Hello." Miranda did not acknowledge her.

Miranda was dressed in a long abstract printed dress in cool jungle colors, and the usual bracelets. Nora stood waiting. This time, the woman would have to open the conversation. Miranda moved forward until she was just two feet away. Her strange pellucid eyes seemed to bore into Nora's like lasers and she shuddered. Why did the woman have such power?

"Max belongs to me, unshriven woman. The portals of hell are opened and thou shall enter on the new moon."

Having spoken this strange, chilling indictment, looking as if she were in a drug induced state or a trance, Miranda turned and left the gallery.

Nora stood as if glued to the spot, head spinning and stomach lurching, threatening to bring up her breakfast. When she could finally move again, she made her way to the phone and punched in Max's personal number at the inn. No answer.

She called the front desk and Melanctha answered. "Martin House Inn, Melanctha speaking."

"Hi, Melanctha,"Nora's voice broke. "You alright, Nora. You sound funny."

"Oh, I'm find, just a little tickle in my throat. Is Max around?"

"No. He took the early ferry over to Hyannis to Trader Joe's and his favorite produce stand. Don't tell the Bartletts. Sometimes the farm doesn't have something he insists he must have. He's a fussy cook, is our Max. Can I help with anything, Nora?"

"Oh, no thanks. Just need to talk to Max. I'll check later."

The phone rang again just as she put it down and turned toward an easel that needed dusting.

"Hello, Gerald Wentworth Gallery, Nora Kavanagh speaking."

"Oh good, you are there. Just wanted to talk. I swear my brain goes through major ups and downs. Lately it's up and I'd love to tell you some things. Are you free later, come have some cold supper with me, dear. I may not be this lucid again for months."

Nora laughed, Adele had a wry sense of humor that never failed to cheer her. "Your memory will be burning bright long after mine has turned to scrambled eggs, Adele."

She was tired from worries about Miranda, but Adele would be just the medicine she needed.

They sat, as usual, on the porch overlooking the harbor. Before them sat a large blue and white platter of cold sliced chicken with a tarragon sauce dribbled over it. A large yellow platter held thick slices of freshly picked tomatoes keeping company with thinly sliced cucumbers dressed with olive oil and fresh chopped basil. Two pitchers dripped with condensation, one of iced tea and one of ruby red Sangria. Nora could smell the pungent rosemary and garlic coming from a basket of hot rolls.

"Adele, this is a sight for sore eyes and a perfect ending to a busy day. Thank you, so much."

They ate pretty much in silence. Adele loved her food and believed that conversation served to dull the taste buds. The last bite swallowed, and Adele was immediately primed for conversation.

"You know that Mabel and I are getting on, dear. Well, when we get together to talk old times we sometimes get it all mixed up. Therefore, I need to tell you how it was so that your young mind can preserve it for when we have gone to the funny farm. I'm having a nice lucid period, at the moment"

Nora smiled but said nothing.

"I know that you know that all three of us best friends, Mabel, Bessie and I, were secretly in love with Simon Graystone. But you have it all wrong about the date of the painting of Viburnum Gate."

Nora wondered what would come next. She had recently recalled how her aunt had once mentioned that she hadn't married young because she made a mistake that left her full of regret. Her aunt hadn't married until she was in her sixties. Was her regret turning down the artist's offer of marriage, she wondered?

"Well, here is how it was, dear. I ran into Simon years after he left the island forever. He had painted all he wanted to here and hadn't made a name for himself. He first went to Boston and had a few shows, then, he was off to New York. We all lost track of him and went on with our lives. Mabel married but Bessie and I did not. Although she did later in life. I never stopped loving him, and when I bumped into him in Greenwich Village in the early forties, he was still dashing. I was still in love with him and he pretended to love me. I moved in with him. I could have rented us a lovely Park Avenue apartment but I knew that would strike at Simon's pride. He'd fallen on hard times. Hadn't painted in years. I devoted my life to him and soon, he took up his brushes again.

I convinced him that if we lived better his clients would put more faith in him. After all, what was my money for but to enjoy life? Gradually, he acquiesced. I bought him fine clothes and we ate in the best restaurants. We partied with the swells. Everything seemed to be going just fine. He was a passionate man. For a time, I truly thought he loved me. The truth was that he never stopped loving Bessie. She kept it a secret from her two best friends when he proposed, his last summer on the island. She refused him because of her father. It would have killed him if she married an itinerant artist rather than old island money. She might have given her father grandchildren with Simon. Instead, she remained childless and broke her father's heart anyway. She never got over that.

"We went back to the island for a little vacation in the summer of forty-one. There was talk of war in the air but we paid little attention. Nantucket seemed like a grand place to spend a month away from hectic Manhattan. Our friends thought we were crazy, but we both knew how special the island was; and so, off we went, driving my wonderful baby blue convertible. I planned to show him off to Mabel and Bess.

"I was off shopping or having tea with old friends, or whatever, when he and Bess evidently bumped into each other in town. The fire was still burning brightly for him; I cannot speak for Bessie. Your aunt was a true beauty, Nora. Botticelli would have been bowled over by her.

"Simon began getting up early and sneaking out with his paints while I slept in. Every day, unknown to me, he was sitting on his little stool, palette in hand, painting Viburnum Gate. Either Bess never saw him or she did not acknowledge his being there, because she never mentioned it.

"When I saw the painting, I asked him if it had been commissioned. Bess's father was still alive and knowing how he cherished that house and the moongate, it seemed logical. Simon was very circumspect and never really answered my question. We returned to New York and over the next few months he became more and more depressed and short-tempered, remaining in his studio all day and into the night. However, he was no longer painting. He'd begin a canvas and then toss it aside…Canvas after canvas, started and thrown aside. He drank himself into oblivion every day. Our social life crashed; I dared not take him into polite society. He never shaved, his hair grew long, and he rarely spoke to me.

"That is why you have so much of his work, Adele."

"Yes, after it happened…Well, first some sherry. "

Adele returned to the porch bearing two crystal glasses. She sat and stared out the window. The wind had come up and little white tops were forming on the waves. A fog had begun to roll in from the Atlantic over sandy Coatue. As if setting the scene for what was to come, the day had grown somber and deadly serious.

"I went into the city to shop for food. Simon was particularly bad. He hadn't gotten out of bed for three days. I thought about calling a doctor, but I knew that would only enrage him. Strange, thinking back, how I stayed with him knowing that he did not love me. Knowing that the reason he had painted Bessie's house was that he loved her with a passion that had thwarted his life…evidently because he had tried to win her and lost.

Nora could not have been less ready for what came next.

"The next day he threw himself out of the window…right after lunch."

Nora's eyes widened so much she could feel the uncomfortable stretch of her lids.

Two days passed in a busy blur as more and more people came into the gallery with paintings they'd found in their attics sure they must be Graystones. Nora treated each one politely, telling them that what they had was lovely, but not a Graystone. Schoolchildren trooped in with their amateur photos of places they thought matched the printouts of paintings. Adele's story had also knocked her sideways. Should she include in the booklet she was putting together for the show that Simon Graystone threw himself out of a Park Avenue apartment window for love of her aunt? A gruesome ending to a talented life, for sure.

It crossed Nora's mind now and then that she wanted to share Adele's story with Max, but work always got in the way. At night, she ate a simple meal, read for a while, and fell into bed, instantly asleep. It wasn't unusual if a couple of days went by without them connecting. Jennie in the mix made for a busier life for Max on top of his inn responsibilities.

Finally, Nora found a small space of time and called the inn. When Melanctha said that Max was still away in America, Nora got suspicious.

"Did he call to say what's keeping him? He doesn't usually stay over there when he goes to shop."

"Nora. God, Nora, I can't do this. I don't know what is going on. This will be the third day with no contact. I'm getting really anxious. He's never done this before. At least, not without checking in with me."

"Three days?" Nora's voice sounded panicked to her although she really had nothing tangible to be panicky about. There had to be a good explanation. "What did he say when he was leaving?" Nora tried to calm herself so as not to add to Melanctha's obvious anxiety.

"Well, *she* came here. That witch he used to be married to, and she made a real fuss. Something about Jennie's summer job. That volunteer thing she is doing with Olivia. He told her he'd take care of it and then she just boiled over. Jeez, I was glad it was after breakfast and everyone had gone. The house was empty and they stood in the front hall. She was screaming at him and he was trying to calm her. Like trying to calm a wild tiger. From what I could hear, she didn't make a lot of sense. She stumbled over her words and sometimes she even sounded like she was speaking in another language. She called him some nasty names and I just slid away into the kitchen and let them go at it. What else could I do?"

"Then, he went to Hyannis to shop?"

"He got her out the front door and came back in. He said he had to go over on the ferry and he expected to be back late. He asked if I could work late and, of course, I said yes. Not as if I have any life but the inn." Melanctha laughed, but it sounded humorless and full of worry.

"By the way, that witch swung at Max trying to hit him in the face. He grabbed her arm, and she shrieked like a banshee. He left, and that's the last time I saw him. He should have called by now."

"Do you know where Jennie is?"

"She's okay, Nora. She's staying at Olivia's to help with her kids. She loves those little tykes of Olivia's and Olivia loves having her there. She's there for a week because, as Jennie told me, her mother is not feeling well. She was feeling pretty well I'd say when she was beating on Max. God, she gives me the willies."

"Jennie told you her mother is ill? Melanctha, do you get the impression that Miranda might be on some kind of drugs that seriously affect her personality?"

"Either that or she is a demon straight out of Hell."

Nora called Adele. "Adele, I know you did a lot of traveling before you came back home to the island to stay. Did you ever, in all your travels, run into any practitioners of Voodoo? Sorry if that is a crazy question but…"

"Nora, no question is crazy. Inquisitiveness is one of the most important traits we can develop in life. So much to learn, so little time. Yes, as a matter of fact, I did. Voodoo? Well, once in Venezuela, I think it was there, although it might have been Jamaica. Well, no matter. I met a man who claimed he could curse anyone for a small price with a money back guarantee if the curse did not take within a month. However, you do know, dear, that such a thing is not so much the work of the practitioner as the work of the mind of the recipient. In order to curse someone and make it stick, you have to plant the idea of the curse in the intended victim's mind. From there, it is like any metastasizing disease. The thought becomes the weapon that injures or kills by overcoming the victim's reason and ability to fight it. The victim must accept that the voodoo can, in fact, bring about a curse. Voodoo feeds on fear, Nora."

It was fear Nora was fighting now. In fact, she'd been fighting it since the day Miranda appeared in the gallery and spoke those enigmatic words that made no sense to her, albeit the tone was abundantly clear. Then, there was the bracelet of tiny white and pink shells left on her porch and the shadowy figure that crept up not knowing that Nora was watching on her own shadow-filled porch.

"So, it really is not something supernatural or other-worldly but just the result of whether the intended victim is weak enough to believe it can work?"

"No, darling Nora, there is nothing supernatural about it. The curses lie in the mind of the beholder. Voodoo is an ancient jumble of hypnotic suggestion, ability to incite fear and sometimes, knowledge of hallucinogenic drugs. Why are you interested in this arcane practice anyway? Not planning on taking it up, are you?"

"Oh, no, just wondering." Thinking quickly she responded, "Just reading a novel that mentions it. Thanks, I guess I really thought that maybe it was some kind of magic and really had power to harm."

At dusk, as the sidewalks filled with people on their way to restaurants, stopping to window shop along the way, Nora locked up and headed for home.

What she longed for was a long, cool bath. But first, she tried Max's cell for what seemed the hundredth time and got nothing. Then she had a brainstorm. The front desk at the Nantucket Inn told her that the manager, Miranda Michelson, was ill and staying in her room. Her first thought was that Max and Miranda were holed up reuniting, blissfully unaware of their jobs and the world outside the room. She whisked that thought away, jumped into her Jeep and headed for the airport.

The ring of her cell phone, lying on the passenger seat, caused her to jump. Her nerves were frayed.

"Hi, Nora. It's me, Jennie. I wonder if I could talk to you? At your house, maybe? Maybe soon?" Nora did not like the sound of the teenager's voice. Jennie sounded both frightened and worried. "Of course, Jennie. I was just heading out but I can pick you up, if you like. Are you at Olivia's?"

Nora turned the car around and headed to Orange Street. Jennie stood on the sidewalk looking a mess. Her hair was uncombed and she'd been crying. Olivia was with her, her arm across Jennie's shoulder.

"You two just take your time. Everything is fine here. When you are finished talking, I have a nice roast in the oven so, come on back for some dinner."

In silence, Nora drove to the duck pond and parked the car. She waited for Jennie to speak. As if awakening from a deep slumber, Jennie looked at Nora and her eyes filled with tears, threatening to flow down her sun-tanned cheeks.

"Jennie, what is it? Please, you can trust me. Tell me what is upsetting you, please."

"You see, Dad won't let me see Mom. I know she's sick. I've known that for a long time…because of that awful old voodoo witch outside of San Juan. If I hadn't been in that stupid accident and worried Mom so much when she thought I might die, she wouldn't have gotten like this. Dad is trying to help her, but he doesn't know how far it's gone. She told me she was going to get him back even if she had to curse you to do it."

Nora took a deep breath and pushed the hair back from her eyes swept there driving in the open Jeep. Before she could comment, Jennie spoke again.

"Sure, I'd love Mom and Dad to be together, for us to be a family. But not that way. We never have been a family until Dad came to stay when I was in the hospital. I didn't meet my father until I was about four. Now that I know him, and I love him, it would be great to be a real family. He's explained why we can't be and I understand. My mother can be scary. I've learned to kind of become invisible when she's like that."

"So, do you think she is on drugs, Jennie?"

"Drugs or some kind of Voodoo spell. Ever since she met that weird lady they call the gray lady, she's changed. Nora, I know Dad loves you. You're…normal."

Nora smiled. "Thanks, for your confidence." She ruffled Jennie's hair and that seemed to calm her a bit.

"Mom has always been a determined person but lately, she becomes obsessed with things. When Dad came to be with me she turned her obsession onto him. She went out to that dirty old shack to that woman to get a charm to help me. Then, when Dad continued to stay and moved into our house, rather than sleeping in the hospital, I think she went back and got something really strong."

"When did you last speak to your father, Jennie?"

"Two days ago. I called my mother's apartment at the Nantucket Inn and he answered. I begged him to let me see my Mom, but he told me that it was best if he had a few more days to get her 'sobered up.' That was how he put it, like she was drunk. I know it isn't alcohol, it's that stuff in the brown crock she got from that awful old witch. She takes it every day, and it makes her strange. She says strange things and acts like she's in another world. I feel like I've already lost her. She kind of goes away."

"Okay, let's make a plan. I think it is best for you to obey Max because he probably has things in hand. I have been trying to reach him and so has Melancthat. Evidently he has his hands full and had lost all track of time. Getting someone down off of drugs is not easy. Maybe he will eventually have to find help, professional, medical help for her. There are plenty of good programs off-island that we might be able to get her into. I have a friend in Boston who works with addicted people. I will call her and try to get some advice that I can pass along to Max in case he is running out of ideas for helping her.

"I imagine he is just keeping her from taking any more and trying to get her to want to get off whatever it is she's been taking."

"I'm going to take you back to Olivia's and I am going to the Nantucket Inn to check on things. Keep your cell on and I will report to you the minute I know something, Jennie."

Jennie hugged Nora tight and Nora hugged her back. She was growing to love this child of Max's, despite her frightening mother.

SIXTEEN

Nora dropped Jennie at Olivia's and remained in the Jeep to make a phone call. Her old college roommate was currently heading up a drug rehab program in Cambridge. After catching up on each other's lives, Nora gave Liza an abbreviated version of Miranda's problem. She left out the Voodoo details, referring only to a drug problem. Obviously, what the old woman in Puerto Rico had given Miranda was a powerful hallucinatory drug. Any other details were irrelevant to the immediate need to get the woman down off of the drug effects.

Liza suggested that the woman be flown off the island A.S.A.P. for treatment. She promised to oversee it herself. Nora told her friend that she'd be back in contact when she knew how the situation was to be handled.

Then she headed for the Nantucket Inn across from Tom Nevers Airport.

The front desk was manned by a good looking Jamaican man who looked more like a lifeguard than a desk clerk. Nora asked for Miranda and was told that she was ill and that her friend Max was caring for her. She then asked if he could contact Max to tell him that Nora was there and would like to meet with him. The young man called an inside number and spoke to someone, hopefully Max, and when he put down the phone, motioned to Nora to go through the arbor to a door at the back of the reception hall.

As she approached the door, it opened. Max slipped out and turned to lock the door behind him. The look on his face said it all.

"Nora. Thanks, I kept meaning to call you and then she'd get dangerous again. She'd hit me with chairs, a copper pot, a telephone and assorted shoes. I'm getting pretty bruised."

Nora knew he was attempting to make light of a horrific situation. She smiled and reached out to hug him.

"She busted both the wall phone and my cell. I knew if I left her alone to go out to the desk that she'd probably kill herself. She's finally sleeping. Every twenty-four hours she comes down enough to sleep. I poured that damned stuff the Voodoo woman gave her down the drain and now she's evidently detoxing. Not a pretty sight."

"Oh darling, Max. You have been living a hell."

"Tell me about it." He smiled and Nora's heart broke for him. He had far more on his plate than anyone needed or could handle simultaneously.

"Jennie came to me. She really needed someone to talk to and trust. She told me about Miranda and that you are trying to get her down off drug addiction. Darling Max, she needs professional help. If only you'd been able to call me, let me in, we could have helped her together. I know she hates me and wants me gone, or dead, or whatever so that she can have you. I know someone in Cambridge, a good, caring, trained professional and she will accept Miranda into the program anytime you are ready to fly her over."

Max's voice, when it came, was like something long strained from overuse. Nora could see that his hands were cut and scraped, as was his face. He had an unattended gash beside his eye that needed cleaning and probably should have had a stitch or two. He was like a battered rag doll, injured but unaware of how and where. Certainly unconcerned with finding help for himself. Miranda had accomplished some things on her agenda. She had taken over his life, his career, his new relationship, and his job as father; at least, temporarily. Fortunately, Nora could put to rest her fears that she had taken over his heart.

"Let's get help and then get you home. The inn is packed and everyone is asking for you. Most of all, Jennie needs her Dad. I'll call for an ambulance. I know the hospital deals with drug cases. What hospital can afford not to these days? All we have to do is leave the arrangements to my friend Liza, who coordinates with hospitals. They will get her over to Cambridge and take good care of her."

Miranda was flown out that night, in restraints and under the supervision of a nurse practitioner from the Nantucket Cottage Hospital whose specialty was drug cases. Max slept at Nora's for eighteen hours. On Sunday morning, Max arose at ten to find Jennie and Nora waiting with warm waffles, blueberry sauce and hot coffee.

"My favorite, how did you know?" Max kissed them both and they sat on the sunny side porch feeling, as Jennie said, "just like a family"

"Thanks, ladies. What would I do without you? When you arrived, Nora, I was at the bottom. I just didn't know what to do next. Then, an angel of mercy showed up, and all was well."

"Oh Dad, I really missed you. Nora is the best. I can see why you love her."

Nora looked at Max and Max smiled over Jennie's head as she hugged him tight. Max hadn't said the words to Nora, but evidently he'd confided the fact to Jennie. That was almost as good. Now however, she wanted to hear them from him. She wanted to say them to him as well.

"Buttercup, would you run inside and get me some more coffee? No sugar, just a hint of cream."

"Nora, come on over here, you incredible woman. I have something I need to say to you. Sorry it has taken me so long. Old wounds, old scars, old fears and trepidations, you know. Time to say…"

But before the words escaped his lips, Jennie reappeared, bearing the fresh cup of coffee and the rest of the pot. "Just in case you need more caffeine to kickstart you, Dad. Hey, I'll be back around three.

Should I come here or to the inn? Tansy, Mary Lou and I are kayaking again. "

"Come to the inn, sweetie, I've got to go and face the wrath of Melanctha. Let's all go out to dinner tonight. You two choose. I'm just so glad to be back to the world, our world; you two can just lead me around like an agreeable hound dog."

They watched Jennie go through the moon gate and down Main Street toward the harbor. Max took Nora's hand and leaned over closer grinning. "Nora Kavanagh, I'm not much of a prize but I'm the best I can be, most of the time. Do you suppose you could love me, maybe a little? I'll settle for whatever you can spare."

"Well, I don't know, I might be too old-fashioned for you."

Max laughed and put his finger over her lips to quiet her. "There are a lot of things I need to tell you over the coming years. That is if you will hang around patiently to hear me out. I've spent a lot of energy trying not to fall in love. Then, you had to come along and captivate me, you vixen. So, to get things started, I guess an old-fashioned girl like you needs to know one thing and hopefully, all else will follow. I love you, Nora Kavanagh. Any chance you might try loving me too?"

Nora did for the next hour, until Max just had to get back to the inn, promising more of the same after dinner.

SEVENTEEN

Nora, Max, and Jennie sat in the lingering twilight on the benches at Children's Beach watching the sailboats bobbing in the light breeze. The three of them had enjoyed dinner at the Brotherhood-Jennie's choice. Olivia had asked Jennie to babysit the next day so she could go over to America for her monthly big grocery shopping. Olivia suggested Jennie spend the night so she, Olivia, could take the early ferry.

"Well, thanks for dinner, Dad. Got to get to Olivia's.

"We'll walk you over there sweetie," offered Max.

"No thanks, Betsey is meeting me on Broad Street. She's coming with me because she's staying with her grandmother next door to Olivia's. Besides, I'm safe walking around here, not like living on that o. i. - Jennie's acronym for other island.

"Well, it is certainly safer here, but don't get too cocky, daughter. You still have to be sensible."

"Always am, Dad. After all, I take after you. See you guys. Now you can get all gooey and romantic."

Max slapped her on her behind saying, "Hey sprout, romance, like fog, happens."

Jennie ran to meet her friend.

Nora and Max passed through the moongate and stepped into a sliver of silvery reflection on the newly- cut grass. Nora had grabbed a morning to mow the small patch that led from the gate to the back porch. The rest can wait, she thought, or maybe die out in the fall and not make any more demands on my time.

"What a night. What a woman. What about making love in that patch of grass over there, love?"

"What about going up to my comfortable queen sized bed with the soft blue silk sheets and making love in comfort free from sand fleas?"

"Good point."

They spent the night together until four-thirty when Max had to head to the inn to start the breads. It had been their most wonderful night, to date. They seemed to be exactly synchronized, every step of the way. Max was a wonderful lover who took his time, he loved to cuddle and exclaimed over the silkiness of Nora's skin. He not only called her "beautiful" but also whispered, "*Cara mia*" into her ears, later telling her he'd read that in a book years ago and always wanted to say it to a woman but never had one inspired him to do so.

They made love over and over, and Max told her that their love was the best ever, and that they would be together in eternity, as well.

Kissing her breasts, he asked her if she wanted children, noting that she was born to give birth.

"Hey, for millennia men have judged a woman's child bearing qualifications by their wide hips and rounded breasts. You, gorgeous woman, were born to be a mother."

"Max Michelson, are you saying I'm hippy? That I need to diet?" Smacking him lightly, more a caress that a hit, she pulled away from him feigning a look of deep offense.

"No love, I am saying that you are perfect in every way, and if some day you decide that you have the time and the interest, well, I wouldn't mind another child. Jennie is my proof of my ability to plant a fine radish. We could make lovely radishes together, naughty Nora. Just let me know."

"I love the score from the Fantastiks, Max. *'Plant a radish, get a radish.'* Maybe we could start a little radish farm right here on the island. We have plenty of room at the house heaven knows. By the way, I'd like to clean out the old summer kitchen and turn it into a studio for Jennie. She really is showing signs of being a promising painter. Have you seen her latest stuff? Wouldn't it be great if some day she could show in the gallery? Also, what about changing the name of the gallery to the Kavanagh-Michelson Gallery? Nice ring to it.

"The only ring I want to see is one on this lovely tanned finger. Wait a minute. What did you just ask me, sweetie?"

"Gerald called to say that he'd like me to have the gallery. I mean, he will sign it over to me. Of course, it is just his name and reputation. I will have to pay the rent and utilities." She smiled at Max enjoying his delight in the news.

"That's top draw, as they say in British movies. Really, top draw. So, I get my own inn and you get your own gallery. Reasons to celebrate, I'd say. How about scrambled eggs and champagne?"

Max took over the kitchen telling Nora, "You savage woman, you drained out all my strength. Need food. Need succor."

The next two days flew by in a flurry of preparation for the retrospective. Nora had stirred up so much interest, she was getting calls from art magazines across the country. The show was mentioned on Facebook and Twitter and the inns and B&B's were all filled up for the weekend of the opening.

Nora was both excited and nervous. The collection she'd assembled of long unseen paintings, not only of the island, but Boston and New York scenes as well, would establish her reputation in the island art scene. She was still awaiting delivery of two paintings. One from Indiana where it had been found in the attic of an old farmhouse and the owner had no idea of how it got there. Another was due from California from a collector of bucolic scenes whose collection included everything from Old Masters to contemporary. He had just happened to buy a Graystone that a friend had unearthed in the storeroom of a New York gallery, although he knew nothing of the painter or its provenance.

He told Nora, "It just spoke to me." While vacationing on the island, he'd seen the ads for the retrospective and took a close look at his own collection.

The *Inquirer-Mirror* had outdone themselves covering the growing excitement and had uncovered even more details of Simon's life that she had not. Deep in the bowels of the paper's archives, one reporter had pulled up two articles that covered local shows of Graystone's work.

She hadn't seen Adele in a week, although she knew her new friend would be there on opening night. Only Max, Nora, and Adele would ever know the full story. That was the way Adele wanted it. "Otherwise, photos of me in my reckless youth will be posted all over People magazine next to that Brangelino couple."

The morning of the opening night, the U.P.S. delivery man came in the front door carrying two large flat packages just as Nora arrived to get set up the tables and chairs. She opened the one from the farm attic in Indiana and stood back to admire it...Max's inn. Once the Hussey homestead and later bought by the Martin family and turned into an inn. Max had renamed it the Spindrift Inn explaining to her, although she already knew, that "spindrift is sea spray, the foam or vapor created by spitting waves." A perfect name considering the vapor they had fought their way through to their final place of peace and contentment. She couldn't wait to show it to Max. The farmer had said that he didn't want it, so she could sell it and send him the money. This painting would remain in the family, she said to herself as she placed it on an easel.

Jennie burst in, taking Nora by surprise. Nora took the girl into her arms. "What, Jennie, are you hurt?"

"No. Mom called, and she wants to get out of there right away. She begged me to come get her. Oh, Nora, she still sounds awful. I don't think it is working. What should I do? I don't want to bother my Dad because he has a house full and he's out straight. I think it's a wedding."

"It's alright Jennie, these things take time and your mother is a strong woman, so she is both bound to fight it. I will talk to Liza at the hospital to see how they are dealing with this. She called you because she knows she can't call your Dad. Just turn off your phone and try to relax. How about doing some work for me? I sure could use an extra hand. There's so much yet to be done before seven.

"Sure, I'd love to. What do you want me to do?"

"Even though the reception tonight won't officially start until this evening, I am putting out some refreshments for whoever comes in during the day. The paintings are drawing a lot of attention. I thought about closing for the day, but that seemed unfair. Some people are day-trippers who have to catch the ferry before tonight. I want them to enjoy the show too."

They spent a great day together, while Nora was talking to customers, Jennie kept an eye on the refreshment table, refilling when things got low. In addition, Nora had asked her to answer the phone and take messages. No time for interruptions on that crucial first day of the retrospective. Anyone interested in purchasing was told that certain of the works were definitely not for sale but others were, although no paintings could be taken away until the end of the month when the show officially ended.

Adele was the owner of the largest number of pieces. She still had not decided what, if anything, she wanted to part with. There was a lot of interest that first day in ten of Adele's. She would not pressure her, but it would certainly make a nice profit for her gallery. Nora smiled to herself thinking that the gallery would be hers once papers were signed. It brought her back to the day just before Christmas two years ago when she came over to sign legal papers to make Aunt Bessie's house hers. It seemed light years ago. So much had happened in the intervening months. Never had she imagined she'd have a readymade family as a result of giving up her life in Boston for permanent residency on Nantucket.

Finally, it was seven, and Max, Jennie and Nora stood together, all dressed up and greeting multitudes of people anxious to get a look at the long lost paintings. Many remarked on what an accomplishment it had been for Nora to have gotten the entire island involved from schoolchildren to the elderly.

One man shook her hand vigorously saying, "My wife hasn't cleaned our old attic in forty years. It's now my hideaway. My son dragged my old lounge chair up there, and I hide when Maggie has her lady friends over for tea." The elderly man laughed and his wife gave him a jab in the ribs.

Three hours later, exhausted but thrilled at what they had managed to create, and the sales on the books that would tide Nora over for a good long time, despite the coming slow season of winter, they grinned at each other. Drooping from three hours of talking, shaking hands and answering questions, Nora nevertheless felt as if her new life had officially begun.

Max and Jennie bustled around clearing tables and picking up errant wine glasses. "Hey Dad, here's one in the potted palm. Do you think the plant had a nice drink of wine?"

Max passed by Nora, holding six wine glasses. He leaned in to kiss her bare shoulder. "You did it, love. Everyone loved it. You've made a name for yourself on the island. I am so proud."

Everything cleaned up and the paintings straightened, Jennie asked if she could go because there was a kayak race the next morning from the Creeks to Coatue and she was determined to win. "Gotta get a good night's sleep. This gallery business is tiring." She smiled and kissed her father and Nora.

"I cannot imagine racing kayaks. Why didn't you choose something like sailing, baby."

"Cause that's for old timers like you, Dad."

Max helped Nora finish up and then they locked the front door and stepped out into the warm night. "Let's not go home just yet. Let's sit on the beach."

"Okay, sure, although I might just nod off."

Longtime island residents Jerry Stiller and Anne Meara stopped them to thank Nora for the "great show."

They met Bill Macy who was out with his new lady friend, the jeweler from a new shop on South Wharf. They had been the first to arrive at the show and then had gone on to dinner. Nora was so happy to see him with someone who obviously shared her feelings for him. As they passed out of earshot, Nora said to Max, "Bill is such a good man, if I hadn't fallen for you, I might have chosen dear, sweet Bill."

"He would have been less of a stress factor in your life, love."

"Oh, well, Max darling, one woman's stress factor is another woman's pure joy and delight. Of course, only a totally whacked out woman would see it that way." She grinned, and Max grinned back.

Nora and Max sat cross-legged and barefooted on the still warm sand. It had been an exceptionally hot day and Nora had worried that the weather might keep people away. Luckily, she'd been wrong. By evening, the Atlantic breeze had taken the curse off the day and brought people in cool and happy.

As Max put his arm around her shoulder, Nora shivered.

"Sweetie, what? Goose walked over your grave, as my mother used to say?"

"No. Nothing really. Well, actually, I just thought about how I might not be sitting with you here after a successful show if Miranda had succeeded."

"But she didn't. Jennie and I are going to see her next week, just before school starts. Liza thinks Miranda will be okay to return to Puerto Rico in a few weeks. I told Jennie we could buy her some classy Boston outfits for school after we visit Miranda."

"I know. All will be well. All is already well. Aunt Bessie always told me not to worry about 'what ifs.' Hey, I forgot to tell you, Adele cornered me just before closing to tell me that she will sell all but the natural spring out at the Moors where she first met Simon Graystone. She told me she chose to sell because it is time to close the door on the past."

"Her story is pretty heart wrenching. I watched her walking around the room, leaning on her cane, gazing at the pictures almost spellbound. I imagine she was recalling the old days and her love for Simon. Everyone loved looking at her albums. Nice addition. She's a tough, adaptable woman, Nora, an example for us all."

"Imagine coming home to find her beloved having jumped from the window. How do you get over something like that?"

"By being wise and knowing that life goes on, even after terrible things occur. She is a survivor. Miranda is a tough survivor. She will be alright now, I know it."

"Good. She's Jennie's mother and is loved. She talks about someday going back for a visit. Time will tell."

Max pulled Nora down beside him on the warm sand and began nibbling on her left ear. Only the sand fleas, happy to find warm human flesh to dine on, sent they back home to Viburnum Gate.

Lying in Nora's bed, Max reopened an earlier, left hanging question. "About that baby we sort of discussed. Do you think we could just be happy to have our delightful Jennie? At our ages, decrepit old things that we are, maybe we ought to think about enjoying these precious years with Jennie and then, when she has gone off to college, do some traveling. A baby would mean eighteen years of parenting at a time when maybe we ought to focus on us."

"Sounds like a plan. A few more years of hard work and we can hire capable managers and maybe go trekking across the Sahara or climb Mt. Everest."

"I was kind of thinking of renting a villa in Tuscany or Provence. Drinking red wine all day, making love all night, and dipping into the Mediterranean periodically."

"Wimp."

"Guilty as charged. Wait here, I have something for you."

Jumping back into the bed holding a small silver wrapped box tied with a green ribbon he held it out to Nora.

"This may have come from your family, the island Folgers. Very likely, in fact. My grandmother, who gave my mother up for adoption, left this in the care of her adoptive parents with instructions to give it to her, Laura, on her twenty-first birthday. It is obviously very old. I had the jeweler check the prongs to make sure they are not going to let go and drop the stone forever to be lost.

He assured me that it is one of the finest pieces of gold work he's seen. He says it is from the turn of the century but that it has seen little wear. Thus, the strong prongs."

Nora opened the box to find a deep blue sapphire set in filigreed gold like lace hugging the square stone. "Makes me proud to be an old-fashioned girl, Max, love."

"My old-fashioned girl. Will you do me the honor of being my wife? I can ask the Woodwards, if you like, for permission. Probably though, at your advanced age, still being single, you can answer for yourself." With that, the wrestling began that included lots of giggles and kisses. Not the norm for a wrestling match, but perfect for the two of them.

"Hold it. I give. Time out. You haven't answered my question. Just in case you did not understand, let me put it another way."

Nora lay still, knowing what was coming, and what she would answer.

"How about marrying a warty old toad who, hopefully, has metamorphosed into a prince?"

Nora's "Yes" sounded choked, but only because she was fighting back tears of joy.

Cynthia Gallant-Simpson began her writing career as a journalist for a small, south of Boston, daily newspaper. From there, because she and her husband are dedicated sailors, she moved on to writing sailing, cruising and galley provisioning and recipe articles for U.S. and Canada cruising magazines. She was educated in Boston and Cambridge, Massachusetts as well as attending a small college west of London, England. It was during her time in England that she became "addicted" to British mysteries and later added cozies to her list of favorite reading material. She is also a painter of Maritime Narrative Americana Primitives full of the ships, whales, lighthouses and mermaids. Relying on the combination of her lifetime love of maritime history, lots of research, and what she refers to as her "Historic eye" she slips back into the days of "Iron men and wooden ships." Her work has been shown in fine galleries and is in private collections from Nantucket and Cape Cod to New Zealand and Europe. One piece resides in the permanent collection of the Tokyo, Japan National Art Gallery.

She is the author of numerous adult mysteries, illustrated children's books, two chapter books for middle readers and her beloved cozies. She has two cozy series available on-line, the India Street Nantucket series and the Liz Ogilvie-Smythe series set in Provincetown on Cape Cod.

In 2005, she and her husband sold their antique Cape Cod sea captain's house and everything not required for living on a forty-four foot boat, thereby simplifying their lives for their shared pursuit of writing and her painting. With friends and family still on Cape Cod, their summer "home" is their boat moored in Pleasant Bay. Winters are spent in warmer climes.

A Deadly Snow Fall
A Deadly Chocolate Pi
A Deadly Fish Tail

India Street: Case of the Killer Scallops
India Street: Case of the Loaded Goose
India Street: Case of the Lethal Escargot

Made in the USA
Middletown, DE
17 August 2023

36847473R00115